A River to Die For

The Fifth Something to Die For Mystery

Radine Trees Nehring

Radine Trees Nehring

St Kitts Press Wichita KS

PUBLISHED BY ST KITTS PRESS
A division of S-K Publications
PO Box 8173   Wichita, KS 67208
316-685-3201   FAX 316-685-6650
stkitts@skpub.com www.StKittsPress.com

The name St Kitts and its logo are registered trademarks.

This novel is a work of fiction. Any references to real people and places are used only to give a sense of reality. All of the characters are the product of the author's imagination, as are their thoughts, actions, motivations, or dialog. Any resemblance to real people and events is purely coincidental.

Edited by Elizabeth Whiteker
Cover illustration by Cat Rahmeier
Cover design by Diana Tillison

First Edition 2008

Library of Congress Cataloging-in-Publication Data

Nehring, Radine Trees, [DATE]
   A river to die for / Radine Trees Nehring. -- 1st ed.
       p. cm. -- (The fifth Something to die for mystery)
   ISBN 978-1-931206-02-0 (pbk. : alk. paper) 1. McCrite, Carrie
(Fictitious character)--Fiction. 2. Buffalo National River (Ark.)--Fiction.
3. Camping--Fiction. I. Title.

PS3614.E44R58 2008
813'.6--dc22
                                        2007043636

Advance Praise for
A River to Die For

"The next best thing to pitching your tent beside Arkansas's beautiful Buffalo River is reading Radine Trees Nehring's evocation of a camping trip that gets dangerously out of hand. *A River to Die For* puts you right there in one of the many caves that pocket the limestone bluffs, and Nehring's love for Arkansas shines through."

—MARGARET MARON, internationally acclaimed author of two mystery series as well as short stories and stand-alone novels

"After exploring the Buffalo National River region for three decades now, it was a thrill to be taken on this mystery/romantic suspense twist around a national treasure I know and love."

—CHUCK DOVISH, producer, writer, and host of *Exploring Arkansas* on Public Television

"Nehring's book is as wild a read as a splash down the rapids of the Buffalo National River in a land that is thrilling and often mysterious. Her descriptions of the river's historic sites are accurate. The author is an obvious river rat with an eye for detail."

—FLIP PUTTHOFF, Outdoor Editor of *The Morning News of Northwest Arkansas*

Praise for the Something to Die For Mysteries

"Readers will delight in Carrie McCrite, a spunky heroine who faces danger and finds love. A pleasure awaits mystery lovers."

—CAROLYN HART, author of the
Death on Demand and Henrie O mysteries

"Nehring's delightful novel features history and romance with murder thrown in. A winning combination and fun read."

—PATRICIA SPRINKLE, 2005-06 President of Sisters in Crime;
author of the Thoroughly Southern mystery series

"I'm a big fan of novels that are true to a local community and region—those that capture a sense of place and really let me feel the area's pulse. That's exactly what Radine Trees Nehring's superb mystery series does."

—JOE DAVID RICE, Arkansas Tourism Department

Acknowledgments

FIRST, MY THANKS TO Sharon Shugart, Curator at Hot Springs National Park (*A Treasure to Die For*), who introduced me to Dr. Caven Clark and the archeological history of Buffalo National River. Sharon knew I was looking for an archeological background for the setting of my new novel, and she alerted me to the possibilities available along the Buffalo. Without the patient help of Dr. Clark, staff archeologist there, this book could never have happened. In many conversations and e-mail exchanges he helped me see the unseen and also hiked with me to historical sites that opened up understanding of the setting and its possibilities.

At the Tyler Bend Visitor Center, Interpretive Ranger Shane Lind (who appears as himself in the book) became another new friend and steady help. I'm sure neither of us could count all the questions I asked him during many phone calls and my enjoyable visits to Tyler Bend. When Shane Lind wasn't there, Tyler Bend Information Receptionist Terry Traywick answered "the question of the day." Law Enforcement Ranger Tracy Whitaker was also a great help.

Park Historian Suzie Rogers, who once lived at Rush, shared information about the history and current conditions in the ghost town. She, too, was a valuable resource.

Visit http://www.nps.gov/buff for more information.

Thanks to Buffalo River Outfitters at Silver Hill, Arkansas, (near Tyler Bend) for letting me select one of their cabins for Carrie and Shirley to stay in (800-582-2244).

Buffalo River Handbook by Kenneth L. Smith, published by the Ozark Society Foundation, is highly recommended to anyone interested in learning more about the Buffalo National River. It was certainly a help to this author.

I am also grateful to members of the DorothyL List who offered advice about how Rob could leave the hospital undetected, and to Officer David Smith of the Gravette, Arkansas, Police Department for help with matters of law enforcement.

Casey Crocker, Visual Coordinator at the Arkansas Department of Parks and Tourism, located the Chuck Haralson photograph that serves as a basis for the cover art. My thanks to them and to other staff members in the department, as well as to Cat Rahmeier, who created the cover art.

Author's Note

THIS IS A WORK OF FICTION. However, the Buffalo National River and bits of its history shared in the story are very real. The Indian Rockhouse, the area around Tyler Bend, and the ghost town of Rush as depicted in *A River to Die For* may be enjoyed by visitors any day of the year. Other locations of historic, geologic, and picturesque interest abound along the Buffalo, as well as opportunities for trail riding, fishing, canoeing, and hiking.

The high bluff and bluffshelter, cave, mine, and archeological treasures found beyond Rush by Rob and Catherine exist only in the author's imagination and in the pages of this book. The name Shane Lind belongs to a real person, but all the other people living in these pages are imaginary.

For more information contact:

Buffalo National River
402 N. Walnut, Suite 136
Harrison, AR 72601
870-741-5443
http://www.nps.gov/buff

Dedication

To the men and women of the
National Park Service.

Prologue

FLAMES CARESSED THE stone wall, marking it with streaks of black as they rose toward the ceiling.

Flames lit the bronze male bodies in the room, and the flickering light became one with a sound now ululating from thirty or more throats.

Finally, when the fuel was spent and the flames returned to dust, the voices died as if directed by a giant hand.

In the dark, the men left the room, crawling one by one through the narrow opening and out under the starlit sky.

The women sealed the hole, this time lighting the purifying fire themselves while their men stood, alert and watchful, behind them.

It was done. Separating into family groups, the forms slid away through the forest.

Chapter 1

W E'D SLEEP ON the *ground?*"
"Not really, Mom. You can use blow-up mattresses or even cots, assuming you have a large enough tent."

"I don't think so. Folks our age are used to at least the
minimum creature comforts. Like beds. "

Carrie shifted the phone to her other ear and waited in
silence, watching chickadees swoop back and forth from the
forest edge to her bird feeders.

Rob's reply sounded stiff. "That's what we planned.
Tents along the river bank."

"Last time I noticed, Robert Amos McCrite, I didn't
own a tent. Your father never owned a tent. We never slept
on the ground. I don't even want to imagine what it would
be like."

Carrie knew she was babbling and that her surprise—
no, shock—was evident to her very bright college professor
son. *Well, so what. Tent camping? Of all the silly...*

"Just because you haven't tried it doesn't mean you won't
like it. You love nature. You love being outdoors."

"I enjoy watching grizzly bears on television. That
doesn't mean I want to pet one."

"Oh, Mom, we thought..."

"You didn't even like Boy Scouts. If I remember, you only lasted with them about four months. I...oh! You said 'we,' didn't you? We who?"

"Catherine and I and..."

"*Catherine?*"

Rob's heavily expelled breath whooshed through the phone connection. "Yes, Mother, Catherine and I are planning this together. We'll go in May, after my classes finish. We both thought you and Henry would like to join us."

"As chaperones?"

The words popped out before her head had time to process them.

Thank goodness Rob wasn't angry. He began laughing and said, "Not exactly. Just come along and enjoy the Buffalo National River area. I've wanted to visit there for ages. It's interesting to me for many reasons, both professional and personal. I'm sure there will be new material for my History of the American Indian classes. Hands-on stuff. Personal observations, you know."

Carrie could hear the professor tones coloring his voice as he continued. "Beautiful geology. Fossils. Exposed strata, caves, rock shelters. Evidence of human presence dating back to at least the Paleo-Indian—that's ten thousand years ago, Mom."

"I know."

She hadn't known, and was aware she'd replied like some kid in a classroom who wanted to impress the teacher. But that was her normal reaction when her son went professorial.

"There are other features too. Of course the main attraction is the river itself, which is open to canoes and small boats. I understand it winds through spectacular scenery.

Catherine and I want to investigate that."

Investigate? Now he sounds downright stuffy.

"And there's hiking and..."

She could almost hear a trumpeted *Ta-da.*

"...I hear fishing on the river is great, especially for smallmouth bass. I know Henry likes to...oh, someone's at the door. I'm expecting a student who's bringing her research outline for me to check. Hold on a sec."

The knock came just in time. She'd been ready to ask if he and Catherine planned to share a tent—when she could squeeze a word in. But it had been thirty years since she diapered this boy-become-man, and Henry's half-sister Catherine was thirty-four. She supposed their sleeping arrangements were none of her business now, though she couldn't help hoping Rob remembered what she'd taught him. He probably wouldn't understand how mothering made her want to ask him about tent plans, nor would he realize that mothering also kept her from asking.

Tenderness rolled through her as she thought back to when she'd held a newborn Rob for the first time. He was so dependent on her then. Not now.

Returning to the present, she listened to voice sounds coming through the phone, couldn't make sense of the words, and went back to her private thoughts.

How many overt mothering acts had to be dropped as children matured? After kids passed into their teen years, so much about mothering became covert activity. Matter of fact, a few things were necessarily covert by the time a child started school. Baby birds had to learn how to fly solo.

Thinking about motherhood as covert activity made her smile. It was important that she and her son be good friends, and, thank goodness, they truly were.

"Mom? You still there? I'm back. So, why don't you talk

this trip idea over with Henry? He can fish, and spring's a great time for hiking. Not too many bugs yet. The Buffalo's a good area for wildflowers too."

"I really don't think tent camping is our kind of activity, Rob. Thank you for including us, but you're on your own this time."

She didn't add: *And you two behave.*

Unwilling to continue, she said, "Oh, look at the time, I must get dressed, Eleanor will be here soon. She, Shirley, and I are going into town so we can check out a building she wants to lease. Did I tell you Eleanor's thinking about opening a flower shop? When we were planning flowers for my wedding, she said she'd been dreaming about having that sort of business for years."

"Eleanor is going into business? Mom, she must be in her sixties."

"I am aware of that, Robert. People our age aren't exactly dried-up-dead."

"Nope, they sure aren't. They might even be capable of sleeping in tents." He paused, and when he spoke again his obvious enthusiasm had her holding the phone away from her ear. "Hey, Mom, this could be a second honeymoon. Single sleeping bags can zip together to make a big one—really cozy. You two might as well enjoy as many honeymoons as you want, and, after all, you've only been married three months. Three months and...how many days is it? Ten? A dozen?"

For some reason her son thought that was funny, as his laughter told her plainly. Now she wished she'd asked him about his own sleeping bag plans. If she was fair game for improper comments, so was he.

She made a strangled noise that probably sounded like a laugh, and after a pause Rob continued, "Well, you three

gals go have fun now. And talk to Henry about coming to
the Buffalo with us. I'll call back in a couple of days. Henry,
uh, does own a tent by the way. Sounds like a nice one."

"He...*what?* How did you...?" She bit her lip and, thank
goodness, the phone went dead.

When a mechanical voice began chanting "If you'd like
to make a call, please hang up and dial again," she put the
receiver back in its stand, shut her eyes, and wondered how
her face could suddenly feel so hot.

It was a good thing Henry had gone into town to renew
her car license. She needed time to think before she saw
him. It was obvious he and Rob had already made plans for
this Buffalo River trip. One of those guy things, and they'd
had no thought of inviting her input. Carrie slumped in her
chair. She felt the same way she had back in grade school
gym class when softball captains always left her until last
when choosing their teams. Oh, yes, she remembered.

Two men, bonding...and they didn't consider her ideas
necessary to their planning.

Left out.

Those were two words from childhood she wanted to
forget, but here they were again.

And then there was a larger problem she could no longer
avoid. It was time to deal with that, too. It had come into
her life three months and—Rob was wrong—nineteen days
ago.

Larger problem indeed. Thing was, Henry was so *here,*
so hugely, incessantly here. She'd expected to be very conscious there was a large man in her house after their marriage, but on some days he hovered until she wanted to
shove him away and shout, "Go play in someone else's sand
box!" She loved her new husband beyond words, but during the almost seven years between Amos's death and her

marriage to Henry she'd learned to enjoy independence and solitude. Henry, on the other hand, soaked up constant companionship like dry earth needing water. He wanted to be close to her, day and night.

She sighed and sat very still in the chair, head bowed. The only thing moving was a finger that twisted one grey curl around and around.

Well, Henry would sure find enough closeness on a camping trip if the two of them were stuffed into a sleeping bag like bratwurst sausages in a hotdog bun.

Left out. And no space for peace, no time alone, not even in her own home.

Except it was Henry's home now too. That was the problem, as well as the blessing.

Oh! Rob said Henry already owned a tent. Umm. What would that be like? After trying to imagine such a structure and getting stuck on vaguely remembered magazine photos, Carrie headed for the garage. Some of Henry's possessions were stored there. Maybe his tent was in one of those boxes, and now was a good time to see what it looked like up close. The date with Eleanor and Shirley wasn't until this afternoon, no matter what Rob thought her words meant.

Henry's mind was on trucks as he turned down the lane to Carrie's—his and Carrie's—house. Then truck thoughts went to the background while he spent a moment glorying in his new life as a married man. He had a wife who was cute, smart, gutsy, opinionated. Life with her would never be dull. Most important, she loved him. She loved Henry King, flawed though he might be. He missed her right now, though he'd only been gone a couple of hours. He just couldn't get enough of being close to her, his little love.

He wondered what Carrie would think about trading

his car for a truck like one he'd just seen on the used car lot in town. That sweet blue truck sparked a lot of ideas. Only three years old, looked new. If he and Carrie went into town for supper he'd show it to her. If he had a truck, they could haul things like bags of bird seed and landscaping timbers so easily. It would be great for carrying camping supplies.

Only a few more days and he could tell her about Rob and Catherine's camping trip plans. He was saving the news as a surprise for their four-month anniversary. Camping would be a new experience for her and she loved new experiences. Maybe they'd find a tent spot near the river where they could hear water bubbling along over the rocks at night.

Then, early in the morning, he'd fish. He might even catch something big enough to eat. He'd have to clean and cook the fish, of course. Wouldn't ask her to do that. She wasn't much on cooking anything from scratch.

He parked in the drive by the front door in case they did go out for supper, picked up his papers and license plate sticker, and headed into the house.

"I'm back. Had to wait a while, but got it done."

Silence

"Carrie? I'm home." He stopped to enjoy that phrase and said it again. "Cara, I'm home."

Where was she?

He heard a distant thump, then another, and followed the noises through the laundry room and into the garage.

Carrie stood in the middle of storage boxes scattered over the floor where his car would normally be parked. She was pulling a large bundle from one of the boxes.

She'd been searching through his things. Why?

Then he realized what she was tugging on. She'd found his tent, and when she looked up at him, he saw storm clouds.

Huh? There had to be a sensible explanation for the look she was giving him. What...?

Rob! He'd forgotten to warn Rob he was saving the camping trip as an anniversary surprise. He'd already bought her a down sleeping bag as his gift. Rats, she'd probably been talking to Rob, and he'd gone and spilled the beans.

"I found your tent," she said.

"So I see. There was no need for you to go through all these dusty boxes, I'd have gotten the tent out for you. We can set it up in the driveway if you'd like to see how it works."

"Rob told me about your plans to go camping at the Buffalo National River. It seems he mentioned it to you some time ago. You two talked it over."

He studied her face. This wasn't good. She was hurt, maybe even jealous, because he and her son were rapidly becoming good friends and Rob discussed the camping trip with him before bringing her into the picture. Henry's many years of police work had made him pretty good at reading emotions on faces.

"Yes, he called to talk to us about it one afternoon when you were out with Shirley, and I decided to save the news as a surprise for our four-month anniversary. I checked my tent out to be sure it was okay to use and it's fine, but my sleeping bag succumbed to mouse occupation and I threw it out. I've bought new ones that can zip together, and..."

Still looking at her face he stopped, and then said, haltingly, "If you want, that is."

She was just standing there, saying nothing.

"I, uh, thought we'd get blow-up mattresses too. All the comforts of home."

Her look changed. She'd had an idea about something

and it pleased her. "You only need one sleeping bag. I'll stay here."

He felt like she'd hit him with a tent pole. "But..."

"You and Rob and Catherine will have a great time. Since I'm not really tuned into camping, I'd just be a drag."

Henry stared at her and wondered what he should say next. His head had gone suddenly empty.

What to say? Heck, what to think?

At the moment it didn't matter. After giving him a happy smile, Carrie pushed through the boxes and walked out of the garage.

"I'll put that stuff back later," she said as she disappeared into the laundry room.

For a moment he stood in the middle of the garage floor staring after her, thoughts churning. Then he looked around the space where his car would normally be. The blue truck would fit in just fine. He took the car dealer's business card out of his pocket and headed for the phone.

Chapter 2

HENRY GAVE HER a book for their four-month anniversary. It was coffee-table size, and full of spectacular
photographs by Arkansas nature photographer Tim Ernst.
She didn't comment when she noticed many of the pictures
were taken along the Buffalo National River.

As days to May marched past, Carrie's eager anticipation
of a full week alone in her house was lightly dusted with
guilt as Henry continued to say the camping trip wouldn't
be much fun without her. Bless the man, she could tell he
really believed that. She always replied by saying he'd have
a fabulous time once he got there and began fishing and
going on hikes with Rob and Catherine—whom they'd both
started to call "the kids."

After all, he'd been divorced about as long as she'd been
a widow. He must understand there were some benefits to
be found in solitude. Occasional solitude.

She understood those benefits. For sure.

Finally mid-May came. After a last kiss, a stroke of his
hand across her hair, a lingering look from eyes that—darn
the man—still hinted of pleading for her companionship,
Henry was gone to the Buffalo.

He'll have a great time, Carrie thought as she watched the taillights of his blue truck melt into the dawn. While she stood there with his words about the benefits of camping by a river floating around her, the pair of wrens that entertained them at breakfast each morning began their familiar *cheerily-cheerily* from the smoke tree.

She hurried into the house, shutting her door on the sound of wrens.

Back in the kitchen she stared at breakfast dishes. If Henry were here, he'd have them in the dishwasher by now. He always said it was his job to clean up when she cooked. He said the same thing if he'd helped with meal preparation, or, on rare occasions, fixed everything himself. They usually ended up cleaning kitchen messes together, constantly bumping bodies as they vied for space at the sink.

Carrie sighed, poured coffee into her *Mom for President* mug and sat at the table staring out into the awakening light. What now? She'd been so focused on creating this week alone that she'd made no plans for it. It was just...time.

The male cardinal appeared on her bird feeder and began picking up sunflower seeds, cracking them in his strong beak, scattering shells right and left.

She pictured Henry, sitting in his favorite chair last evening, cracking and shelling nuts to eat while he watched television. Her favorites were the almonds, and he often handed her one, putting the empty shell in a blue enamel dish he'd brought here with the rest of his possessions.

Henry was very neat, almost obsessively so. Well, thank goodness for that—she never had to pick up after him. Mrs. Cardinal now...

Where was Mrs. Cardinal? The pair usually came to the feeder together at first light each morning. It was still dark enough that the female's quieter coloring could fade into an overall pinkish dawn, but a careful binocular-assisted study of the area revealed no Mrs. Cardinal. Maybe the pair had a nest with eggs or baby birds and she was tending that. Otherwise she'd be on the feeder with her mate, allowing him to pick out choice seeds and hand—Carrie chuckled—how would you say that? Did birds "beak" instead of hand? Anyway, he'd be sharing seeds, like Henry gave her almonds. Cardinal pairs were noticeably affectionate and usually stayed close together, so there must be a nest hidden nearby.

She'd have to tell Henry about birds doing "beaking."

Enough! She shoved her chair back with a bang and went to clean up the dishes. "After this is done," she said to FatCat, who'd come to sit by her feet with unflagging hope some table scrap might drop her way, "I'll begin cleaning out kitchen cabinets and drawers."

Her voice, loud in the silent house, startled her. Well, for goodness' sake, how silly. She never talked aloud to FatCat, knowing full well that cat could read her thoughts.

Henry cruised into the campground. He'd told Rob to watch for a blue truck, but a quick drive around the area didn't turn up any sign of the kids, or of any humans at all, though most sites held tents or small RVs. Evidently everyone, including Rob and Catherine, was away doing whatever they'd planned for today.

Rob had phoned Blackberry Hollow yesterday afternoon to tell them he'd left his apartment near the university in Norman as soon as he finished lunch and was just then coming around Oklahoma City on the turnpike. He'd be at Catherine's house in Claremore by the time she and her law partner closed their office for the day. They'd switch Rob's belongings and camping supplies to her Jeep, grab hamburgers, and head for Arkansas.

Carrie talked to Rob first, then he did, and both of them urged him to stop over with them for the night. The answer had been an emphatic "No, thanks." Those two were so eager to get started on their vacation that they planned to drive straight through, though that meant they'd arrive at their chosen campground next to the river at Tyler Bend after dark.

Not a sensible plan as far as Henry was concerned. Tents were hard enough to set up in daylight, let alone in the dark, but they didn't seem to care about that. Maybe, if he'd had someone to go camping with when he was their age, he would have seen it simply as one more adventure. His former wife was sure no camper and now Carrie wasn't either. He'd hoped that she... Ah, well, the few times he'd taken a tent on fishing trips, he'd always been alone or with a few other guys, and the kids would add a lot to this trip. Good time for the three of them to really get acquainted.

He wished he'd thought to ask what kind of tent, or tents, they had, so he could locate their spot now. Didn't want to be too close. Didn't want it to seem like he was spying.

It wasn't that he felt protective about Catherine. It was just...well, he'd admit to being a little curious.

A sister. Funny, he'd spent thirty-three years trying to forget she existed, then, whiz-bang, Carrie bugged him about relatives to ask to their wedding and he'd spilled the beans.

He'd said the minimum—his dad's walk-out on his mom and swift marriage to Elizabeth MacDonald, a woman young enough to be his daughter. The baby announcement, formally addressed to Police Lieutenant Henry King, arriving at his office six months later. The shock, the hurt for his mother.

He never let on to anyone that he knew about a baby half-sister born to a woman younger than he was. He said nothing to his mom, nothing to his wife, Irena.

The baby announcement, torn to bits, went in the men's room trash at the police station, and that was that. No more Catherine. She was only trash...*as was her mother,* or so he'd thought for thirty-three years.

Then Carrie, with her curiosity and love for family connections, came into his life. She located Catherine MacDonald King, a lawyer in Claremore, Oklahoma, and invited her to their wedding.

Aw, nuts. He was used to his little Cara and her ways. Now it was time he got used to Catherine. He could do it, especially since it looked as if she and Rob were connecting like he and Carrie had. Weird. His sister, Carrie's son.

There was a polite horn beep behind him. He jerked back to awareness and realized he'd stopped his truck in the middle of the campground road. He waved an apology and drove ahead to a parking area where he could pull off.

Catherine and Rob. What if...

Huh. He'd only been married to Carrie for a little more than five months and here he was, thinking about other people's business just like she did.

Come on, King, admit it. You hope those two will get married, sort of like a seal on the family.

It would make holidays nice. Christmas, Thanksgiving. There would be his daughter, Susan, her husband and son, plus Rob and Catherine, plus...more babies?

Hmmm. If Rob and Catherine had children they'd be Carrie's grandchildren and his nieces or nephews. But should he call them that? He'd be so much older. Phooey, he'd just call them his grandchildren, and they could call him...what? Uncle Grandpa?

He looked at his watch. Moving on toward eleven
o'clock. Time to quit this day-dreaming and get settled.
He started through the campground again, noticing more
details this time. Nice place, nestled here in the river valley.
Bathroom and showers there, even a place for cleaning fish.
Catherine's red Jeep would be obvious if the kids were here.
He looked at each set-up location, wondering if anything
would give away where the two of them were camping.

No clues, but they'd be back for supper. In the meantime he'd find his own spot, and then phone Carrie. He'd
promised to call her as soon as he arrived. She'd asked him
to report on whether Rob and Catherine were sleeping in
one tent or two. If he called now, all he could say was that
he had no idea what their arrangements were. Just as well.
None of Carrie's business. *Nor his.*

He cruised along until he saw an unclaimed spot near
the river, parked, and got out to look it over. Number three.
Paved pad, lantern hook, enclosed grill, area mowed and
neat. Just beyond the tent pad there were trees, brushy stuff,
and scattered white wildflowers outlining the famously wild
and free Buffalo National River. He couldn't see the water,
but he could hear it, and he stood motionless, listening, feeling peace as well as thankfulness for those who had fought
to save this river from a multitude of Corps of Engineers
dams.

The murmur of conversation and muted splash of a
paddle joined the river sounds. A canoe must be gliding
past beyond the trees. There was a space of silence filled
only with the ruffle of water, then the gentled voices floated
toward him again. One male, one female.

A tickle of sorrow stirred in his head. He just couldn't
understand why Carrie didn't want to come here, even after
he offered to find them a cabin somewhere nearby. It was

okay that she didn't like fishing: she could have done something else while he fished. Well, maybe she would have been
bored, and it was true he'd have worried about that.

So, she was just being thoughtful—wanted him to have
a good time at things he enjoyed and she didn't. He missed
her bouncy presence but, well, it was okay.

Over the trees on this side of the river he could see an
exposed bluff above the opposite bank. He'd bet Rob would
be able to tell him all about the rock layers there. He looked
around again. Toilets and showers were maybe a bit far away,
but otherwise this was great. Time to sign in, post his claim
tag, and get out the tent.

Rob vaulted the creek in one leap, turned back and reached
a hand toward Catherine. "Step on that rock in the middle
of the water. Careful, it's probably slippery. Here, take my
hand. Now jump."

She did as he said, landing against him with an *oooof*
that turned into an *ummmm* when, impulsively, he put his
arms around her, cradled the back of her neck in his hand,
and pulled her into a kiss.

She felt warm. This was...nice.

A familiar confusion interrupted his pleasure. Should he
be doing this? He didn't want to mess up here: he wished he
knew what she was thinking.

He stopped wondering when she pushed closer and their
body heat connected from chest to knees. Whew. *Rob Mc-
Crite, why are you are always such a dunce around women?*

Should he run his hand gently down her back, or, uh,
would it be good to say something romantic? Oh, sure,
and what would that be? He didn't have the words, and he
wanted everything to be perfect with Catherine.

She heard the noises before he did, distracted as he was,

and—all too quickly—pulled away from him. Then he heard it too, a rattle of rocks, talking, laughter. There were people on the Rockhouse trail, coming up fast. He turned and hurried away from her, not daring to look back. When the family of four passed them, sending swift *Hello*'s and a *Beautiful day* floating back in the warm air, he and Catherine were yards apart. As they walked, heads down, steps jerky, Rob thought they must look like teenagers caught making out on a field trip.

They hiked in silence for several minutes, concentrating on their footing with more intensity than the terrain demanded.

"So," she said finally, "I guess you know all about this Indian Rockhouse we're hiking to see?"

Drawn out by a question he could respond to sensibly, Rob said, "I know something about it, but only because I did research on the Buffalo National River last winter. It's really a cave with a very wide opening, providing shelter for Indians over thousands of years. Nice place to live. Wide overhang with room for fires. There are springs inside the cave, plenty of water."

"Will you look for Indian stuff, maybe things to take back and show your classes?"

Rob was stunned by her question. He stopped and turned back to face her, and then hated himself for the reproach and even horror that must show on his face. He wouldn't have expected this kind of thinking from someone like Catherine, though he knew it to be fairly common among the general public. It was a wonder that archeologists had anything at all left to study from previous civilizations.

He thought about the robbing of pharaohs' tombs in Egypt and shuddered.

Now she looked confused, and her next words came out

in a stutter. "I-I said something really dumb, didn't I? I just thought...well, because you are a college professor and all... but of course this is a national park, isn't it? Removing stuff is probably against the law. Stupid question, I am sorry." She bit her lip.

"No, no, I'm the one who's sorry. Your initial assumption is pretty natural for a...a...lay person. It's just that, well, I want everyone to respect these places and see their importance as part of our heritage, our history, let alone that you're right, it is against the law to remove artifacts of any kind from a national park and many other locations as well."

He was on fast forward, no longer puzzled about what he should say or do next. "The Indian Rockhouse has been explored by experts as far back as the 1930's as well as periodically looted over the years. I doubt there'd be anything to find, even if I were authorized to search or dig. I just wanted to see it and picture Indian life there."

He waved an arm toward a distant bluff face barely visible through the greening trees. "But, imagine that we hike off this trail, going in the direction of that bluff instead of to the Rockhouse. We fight our way through heavy underbrush, struggle over rocks. When we get to the base of the bluff, we look up and think we see an opening. After a tough climb we can look over the edge into the shelter, and it appears no one has been there for ages. The floor is covered in dust, no footprints. We see fire-marked rocks, some interesting-looking humps and bundles way in the back. Just think what that could mean."

Her brown eyes were wide open as she turned toward the bluff he'd indicated, and her response came quickly. "We've discovered something no one else has seen in hundreds of years."

"Or maybe thousands of years. Imagine it. The leavings

of humans from a distant past are all around us. Catherine, if we as much as move one thing there, we're breaking apart history, removing keys to the lives of ancient people who passed this way. I don't have the tools, the knowledge, or the authority to peel back, understand, and preserve the layers of secrets hidden in a site like that."

"So, what do we do?"

"We climb down that bluff face as fast as we can and hurry to report our find to the Buffalo National River archeologist, Anderson Fletcher. I spoke with him last winter about the possibility of my coming here for learning and research. It was really a courtesy call. I have no intention of doing invasive exploration, just some looking around, sensing the past, if you understand what I mean. I hope to meet with Dr. Fletcher before this trip is over though, perhaps go to his office at park headquarters in Harrison."

She turned back from gazing toward the bluff, and now with a frown wrinkle in the skin between her eyes said, "His job must be both fabulous and frustrating."

Rob smiled. She was getting it! "Frustrating for sure. Like trying to fit a puzzle together when someone has stolen most of the pieces. Site protection is one of his primary responsibilities, but so often it's too little, too late. European Americans have been in this area for well over two hundred years, Spaniards possibly through here long before that. There were white settlers by the 1820's. If something they saw looked interesting to them—chipped stone tools, weapons for hunting or defense, bits of pottery, maybe even the remains of more perishable items like a cradle board—well, they probably took them as a curiosity. They wouldn't have known any better. What's much worse are the thieves who loot these sites for money. They sell artifacts on the Internet and other places. I can't begin to say what I think of them,

I..."

Catherine's frown was gone. Now he saw the beginning of a grin wrinkling the corners of her mouth and said, "Oh, sorry; guess I locked into teaching mode. I get carried away."

"No, no, don't apologize, this is exciting. It's obvious I have much to learn. Rob, I *want* to learn."

He'd turned back to start walking again when he imagined he heard her say, "From you."

Chapter 3

"I COULD LIVE HERE, Rob."

"Oh, come on. This shelter doesn't have a microwave, flush toilet, mattress and springs or..."

"Quit that, you goof. You said you wanted to see the Indian Rockhouse so you could picture Indians living in it. That's exactly what I'm doing. I'm an Indian squaw, or maiden, or whatever the politically correct term for an Archaic American Indian female is now. Thinking as that woman, I declare this a pretty cool place to live. I certainly have a huge living room, though of course I realize I am sharing it with other families."

She looked up at the rough rock surface far above her head. "This ceiling must be at least forty feet high, and the room is, what—about three hundred feet across at the front? I cook game, or fish you've speared, over a fire I build between those rocks back there. See, the smoke goes through that hole in the roof.

"I guess if I've never seen a mattress, I won't miss having one, and besides, my strong brave—that's you—killed the biggest Arkansas black bear he could find, or maybe even a wooly mammoth, so we have a thick fur rug to sleep on.

I've covered the bearskin with soft deer hide. I think I recall from some long-ago reading that the women chewed deer hide to make it soft, especially for their babies. Much as thinking about that could gag me, I won't gag because I'm not Catherine MacDonald King, J.D., I'm...Autumn Moon, mate to...to...Standing Bear. I wonder, did Indians get married back then—have some kind of 'I claim you' ceremony? I think I recall one from *Dances with Wolves*, but of course that took place in more recent history."

She turned her head to look at him, hoping he'd have an answer hinting whether or not his thoughts were on the same track as hers. But Rob McCrite, alias Standing Bear, stared at the ground, stirred dust with a stick, and said nothing.

He was so close. When she turned her head, she almost had to lean back to bring him into focus, and she could smell his heated skin with a hint of smoke from their morning campfire. The rock they sat on was quite small. Did he choose it because of that? There were plenty of bigger rocks in the shelter. When they first arrived, he'd explained those rocks had fallen from the ceiling over the ages, and the only place archeological treasures might be found here today would be under tons of rock.

She waited another minute for his answer. None came. His eyes stayed focused on the ground as he stirred circles in the dust, so she went back to her musing.

"As for the toilet? Hmmm..." She waved an arm in a wide sweep around the woods in front of the cave opening. "Far away from this entrance, of course, and I promise to bury anything I leave. You just chip me a nice little digging tool out of a piece of rock. Okay, Standing Bear?" She touched his side with her elbow and he jumped.

"Okay, Standing Bear?"

He was blushing. After another minute of silence he said, "Sorry, I've been lost in imagining we lived here while you were talking about it. Sorry."

"You said 'sorry' twice, and one was too many, Rob. No need to apologize. We were imagining together, that's all. I...I...did Indians ever kiss?"

Again he offered no response, and she was beginning to wish she'd kept her imagination to herself and her mouth shut when he stopped stirring dirt, put his arm around her, and touched her cheek lightly with his lips. She moved her head around until their lips were together and, after a moment, heard a tiny groan from one of them. He dropped the stick, circled her body with both arms, and began a kiss that created new imaginings.

Carrie picked up another toothpick and continued poking at almost invisible flecks of dust and dried food in the tiny indentations on her stove's control knobs. Stupid design, nothing but decorated dirt collectors. She attacked the next handle as viciously as if she were fighting wildcats, then yanked the knob completely off and took it to the sink for a good scrubbing. Goodness knew what minute organisms might be hiding in those slots. She'd write the company a letter suggesting a smoother design. Why hadn't they the good sense to...oh. Her *irate housewife* mood shifted into reverse when she remembered that smooth knobs could slip in your hands when you tried to turn them.

Ah, well.

Henry fired up the propane stove, turned it to low, and set the stew on to heat. He and Carrie had put together a big pot of beef stew yesterday with the thought he could warm it up for supper for the kids and himself his first night here.

There was still enough left in the refrigerator at home for a couple of meals. In fact, when he talked with Carrie just a few minutes ago, she said she planned on having stew tonight.

She also told him she'd spent the day cleaning and organizing the kitchen. Odd. He was very sure the kitchen didn't need that. After he moved in last Thanksgiving, he bought dividers and re-organized their more frequently used silverware and kitchen tools—with her permission, of course. Things could get out of order when you lived alone, and it was easier for him to find tools when they were in order. But they'd both done a good job keeping everything organized and squeaky clean since then. So, why all the cleaning now? A whole day of it?

He stopped pondering this when he noticed a red Jeep coming into the campground. His was the third camp site from the entrance so the kids saw him right away and pulled in.

"Hey, Henry," Rob said as he hopped out of the Jeep and hurried to shake Henry's hand, submitting to a bear hug instead. Catherine stood apart watching them, until Henry—figuring he had to be fair—reached out and pulled her in for a cautious hug.

After a quick wash-up the kids helped put out fruit, crackers, and bowls of stew, all of which vanished in a hurry. When they'd cleaned away the dishes, the three of them sat in Henry's lawn chairs while Rob and Catherine told him about their day, spent hiking to various bluff shelters in the area. Occasionally during the telling one of them would hesitate, leaving the other to pick up the story.

Rob described the long hike to the Indian Rockhouse and what they'd seen along the way: an old mine shaft, high waterfall, Panther Creek, a sink hole into some unknown cave, lots of wildflowers. He faltered into silence when he came to their arrival at the cave.

"When we got there," Catherine said, "it was easy to imagine we were Indians from centuries past, living in that place. Rob has told me so much about American Indian history that he makes it natural to picture their lives." Her eyes glowed with pleasure as she looked over at Rob, who had fallen silent. "It was loads of fun. We'll have to show it to you before the end of the week."

"What are you planning tomorrow?" Rob asked. "Do you want to go exploring with us?"

"No, thanks," Henry said. "I'm eager to begin fishing. It's been a couple of years since I tried my hand, and I've missed it. Think I'll get up early and do some casting from the banks, see what comes in on the line. Maybe we'll have fish for dinner tomorrow night. If not, I have plenty of hot dogs in the ice chest."

"We don't have many perishables with us," Catherine said, "so yes, let's eat your stuff first. We can start on the canned goods later in the week."

Rob stood. "Time to go for showers and turn in. Thanks for the terrific meal. Mom makes a mean stew, but I detected a new zing, and I imagine you had something to do with that."

Henry was chuckling when Rob continued, "We'll see you for supper tomorrow evening. We plan on driving over to Rush in the morning—take a look at some of the old zinc mines and what's left of the historic town. After that, who knows? Might see about renting a canoe and putting it in the river."

"Do you want me to pick you up somewhere? I bet we could tie a canoe in the back of my truck."

"No need, the people who rent the canoes provide that

service. Thanks, anyway."

After goodnights were said, Henry watched them drive around the campground to the opposite end, pull in, and park. Two small tents huddled there, side-by-side.

Ah, he thought, *my family.*

Not long after he and Carrie met, he told her he had no living relatives. Now, because of her detective work, he'd gained a newly-discovered daughter with a husband and son, plus a half-sister. Then there was Carrie's son Rob, and Carrie herself—*his wife*.

A new thought struck him and he laughed aloud. It was a good thing he and Carrie were too old to have children. She'd already given him a family of six, and all within a year.

Too bad she wasn't here so he could thank her appropriately.

Chapter 4

G HOST TOWN FOR SURE," Catherine said as the Jeep bounced along on the rocky road. "Just look at those houses! The term *cozy* does *not* come to mind. I would prefer accommodations in the Indian Rockhouse—at least it's weatherproof." She sighed as loudly as she could. "But if we *must* admire these, admire them we will."

"Well, uh, if you'd rather do something else..."

"Oh, you sweet goof, I'm just joking. Go ahead and read what it says in the flyer that guy at the visitor center gave us. I'll slow down so we won't miss seeing anything."

He was staring at her again, so she continued, "Don't mind me, I get silly sometimes."

After a space of silence Rob opened the flyer and began reading: "'*The houses in this row date from about 1899. They are built of a simple board and batten construction; clapboard siding has been added to some.*'" He paused and looked at her as if he expected a comment.

"Okay," she said, trying to be properly sober, "but they sure look derelict. Miners' homes, I guess?"

"Doesn't say. Shall I go on?"

"Waiting for your next words, breathless and all a-twitter."

Oh-oh, that just slipped out. She resisted the urge to clap
her hand over her mouth.

"'*In the* 1880's *farmers on Rush Creek discovered zinc ore,
and soon the rush to Rush began.*'"

"Well, what a cute turn of phrase."

"Perhaps," he said, "but I've found such word playing
often helps my students remember what I'm telling them."

"My apologies, Professor. I really will be quiet. Tell me
first though, what does one do with zinc?"

"A lot of things—I'm only sure of a few. It was used for
making photographic plates back then, and in batteries and
paint. During World War I, they'd have wanted it for brass
bullets since zinc is a component of brass. It's also important
in the galvanizing process."

"Somehow I just knew you'd be able to expound on the
subject," she said, then made a vow to stay silent for at least
the next ten minutes. He was acting like a professor, she
should act like a lawyer—reticent and wise. Rob McCrite
was obviously not ready for her silly side.

Rob felt as if his brains were leaking out somewhere. Was
she making fun of him? Surely Catherine wouldn't have
agreed to this trip if she didn't at least like him. The kisses...
He stirred in his seat, remembering those kisses. There were
also friendly looks, hints she enjoyed being with him, and
two agreeable weekends spent together while they'd explored
first Claremore and then Norman, Oklahoma.

She was so...different. And yet, come to think of it, his
mother was kind of different too, and the fact that he often
didn't understand her hadn't bothered him for years.

He sure wanted to be on Catherine's wavelength. Trouble was, he couldn't figure out how to get there. Maybe it

just took a lot of time—like with Mom.

"I probably told you more than you wanted to know," he said, "about zinc, I mean."

"Not at all. I asked, you told me. Lawyers aren't exactly famous for understatement, either. So tell me about these buildings we're passing now."

"Let's see, where were we? Ah. *'By the 1890's the mining boom was well established.'* According to this, the heyday for mining was during World War I, *'with all the mines in full operation, producing zinc for the war effort.'*" He studied the map in the flyer and pointed to a numbered dot. "Here's where we are." He looked up and checked their location. "The building we're passing was the Taylor-Medley Store. It's in pretty bad shape, isn't it?"

"Yep, more splinters than substance. Still, you can tell what it was. Looks like the general stores in western movies. Easy to picture cowboys—or here I guess it would have been miners—watching the town's action from that porch."

"On our left," Rob continued, "the huge fireplace and chimney? Flyer says it was part of a smelter. And there, under all the weeds and vines, is the stone foundation of Hicks' Store, built in 1916."

"Hm," she said, slowing the Jeep. "Too bad it's gone. Just parts of a couple of walls. I'd say neither store has seen a customer in many decades, but they prove that Rush was once prosperous enough to support at least two retail establishments. Aren't they sad-looking now? The whole town is sad-looking."

He laid the flyer aside, shifting comfortably into teaching mode. "Ken Smith talks about Rush's early period in his *Buffalo River Handbook*. I bought it at the visitor center yesterday and skimmed through the part about Rush last night."

"That explains why you had your lantern on so late."

"Um-hmm. Anyway, Smith says the town had over two thousand inhabitants during the period of full-scale mining. A real boomtown. There were plenty of the problems one tends to expect in mining towns. He mentions bar fights involving both men *and* women, and bootlegging."

"Tsk, tsk," was all she said.

"After the war ended, mining wound down, and soon Rush was shrinking, with fewer and fewer people and businesses. Some of the processing mills were dismantled for scrap during World War II. There was an attempt to revive mining in the late 50's and early 60's, but I guess that didn't amount to much because it fizzled out and the town pretty much died."

She paused in the entrance to a parking lot at the end of the road. "Enough history for now. Let's go see the river and the mines."

He picked up the flyer again. "They have warnings about the mines. It says an inspection in 1984—quote, *found hazards including loose ceiling rock, deep pits, and tunnels showing signs of recent cave-ins...human entry into the mines is strictly prohibited.*'"

She peered up at him from under dark lashes, stuck her lower lip out, and said, "Not even a teeny peek inside?"

Startled, he stared at her, and then recovered. "I think not. They make it clear going in the mines isn't safe. Besides, they're now bat sanctuaries."

"Aw, shucks, Dr. McCrite, I wanna look for zinc."

She started giggling, and this time he laughed with her, but the comment bewildered him. What she said often did.

The parking lot held several cars, but there were no people in sight. Catherine twisted the steering wheel sharply and pulled her Jeep in between a truck and an old van with a boat rack on top. "Why are all these cars here?" she asked. "I haven't seen a single person since we got to Rush, and I'm not in the mood to muddle through a crowd. I'd hoped we'd have the area to ourselves."

"The cars probably belong to day hikers and canoeists. When people bring their own canoes, it would make sense to use two cars and leave one here, another at their start or take-out point."

They walked down a gravel ramp toward the shoreline. Catherine, eager to see the river, hurried ahead and came around the curve above the canoe landing first. "Oh, the water color is so beautiful here, just *look* at it, Rob. Teal blue, even brighter than your mom's eyes. It appears dyed, not like the softer greens at Tyler Bend."

"Same water, though," he said. "I believe the different coloring is caused by the way light reflects off bits of minerals in the water. It is rather like Mom's eyes."

She looked up at him. "And your eyes are the green we see at Tyler Bend. Did your dad have green eyes?"

"I don't know, maybe."

"You're not sure about the color?"

"They might have been green," he said. Then, as if afraid that sounded inadequate, added, "He wasn't home a lot. His law practice...I don't know about the hours you keep, but he argued many cases that required long preparation. They were often the kind of criminal cases you read about in newspapers. He was really dedicated to his work."

"Well, I enjoy practicing law, and sometimes I work long hours, but not to the degree a big-name criminal law-yer might. I am taking a vacation with you, right?"

"My dad never took a vacation in his life. Only those short hunting trips with the friend that...that...oh, God help me, with the friend that killed him." He was silent for a moment, then said, "I made a mistake. I said *friend*. That's a profane misuse of the word."

He stopped walking and turned to look out over the river before he continued. "I told you about it, didn't I? The stockbroker *friend* who cheated his clients? Dad began to suspect what was going on and confronted him. The man shot Dad when they were hunting together. It was well planned to look like an accident. We had no idea what really happened until about a year and a half ago. Henry's daughter Susan works for the same firm that Dad's killer did. Something in the records made her suspicious, and she found all kinds of stolen investments. If it hadn't been for Susan, Mom would still be struggling financially."

"Yes," she said softly, "you told me. I'm sorry." She touched his shoulder, and they stood together in silence for a time before moving on down the slope.

At the river's edge they watched two couples launch canoes. After the canoes slid out of sight around a bend, Catherine headed along the shore to the strip of shingle bordering Rush Creek. She heard Rob's footsteps crunching behind her and said, "Listen to the creek. It's saying 'bubble-rattle-swish, bubble-rattle-swish.' It sounds happy to be joining the river."

She bent and picked up a walnut-sized rock. "Look at this, it's like a sponge." She peered at her find. "Fossils. Must be the remains of more than a hundred tiny creatures here." She held her hand toward him, cradling the rock.

He cupped his hand under hers, and she studied his face while he studied the porous-looking rock. Finally he said, without looking up, "All of the Ozarks was part of a Mississippian era sea some three hundred and fifty million years before our time. These fossils are the remains of creatures in that sea."

She left her hand nestled in his as she said, "While I'm holding it, I feel connected to all life—from these tiny creatures to me, Catherine King, here right now."

At that he did look at her, a slight smile on his face. Then he cleared his throat and said, "Shall we go for a hike? We can come back to the river later, maybe eat our lunch sitting here by the creek."

He took his flyer out again and opened it to the trail guide, moving a finger along as he spoke. "How about walking along this old road to the White Eagle Mine trail first? We can climb the hill and explore the land above Rush and Clabber creeks."

Catherine looked at the map. "Why go clear up there? The map doesn't have any features marked, and it looks like the park boundary cuts through the area." She pointed.

"So much the better. We'll be in uncharted territory."

They followed the two-track road for about fifty yards and then turned off into a gravel parking area. It was surrounded by lush growth including hundreds of small lavender daisy-like flowers. When Catherine stopped to look at the flowers, Rob said, "Western daisy, according to Carl Hunter's guide to Arkansas wildflowers."

"I need to get a copy. I saw them at the visitor center."

They came to crumbling concrete piers, the remains of an ore processing mill, according to the map. A vintage silver Thunderbird convertible, top up, sat near a pile of mine tailings beyond the piers.

Rob went to inspect the mill remains while Catherine walked around the Thunderbird. She could hear the slight *tink* of its cooling engine, but didn't dare put her hand on the hood to see if it felt warm. The owner might show up suddenly and find her touching his—or her—baby. Worse, she'd probably leave fingerprints on the polished surface.

Then she noticed that the owner—or someone—had left dusty smudges on the trunk lid. Too bad. Spoiled an otherwise pristine surface. Unconsciously she wiped her hands on her jeans and imagined what it would be like to sail along the highway, top down, in such a car.

Rob's voice called her back to reality. "Catherine? Shall we look for the mine?"

Hearing intensity in his voice, she decided now was not a good time to share her car dreams. She left the beautiful Thunderbird behind and followed Rob, scrambling over the pile of mine tailings, then up a worn trail until they reached a cave-like hole in the hillside. The mine opening was blocked by horizontal metal bars welded to a framework bolted in rock around the mine entrance. A rusted-out mine car with no wheels hunched on the ground beside the bars.

"We won't see much here unless we can turn into bats," Rob said.

Honoring what seemed an attempt at humor, she laughed, but he was already climbing again and probably hadn't noticed her laughter. *Oh, well, march on.*

From then on the climb grew steeper and increasingly rough, much rougher than yesterday's hike to the Indian Rockhouse. She began lagging behind, wondering if he would ever stop for a rest. When the trail branched near a rocky outcropping Rob did stop, but only to study each arm of the trail while she leaned against a tree, puffing. He said something she couldn't hear and finally turned around, looking startled when he saw her some distance below.

Talk about the absent-minded professor. Had he forgotten she was here?

"I'm for taking this trail to the right. It's much fainter,

less traveled. Okay with you?" He sounded excited, fired up by his quest for what was, as far as she knew, an unknown goal.

Rob McCrite, explorer. This is his passion, Catherine. Get used to it. You came on this trip with your eyes open. You knew he was a college professor, more in love with his field of learning than with any fellow human, except maybe his mom. You admired that. He has a focus similar to what you feel for the law, and you thought maybe, this time, you'd met someone who...

"Okay?" He repeated. "I'll go on. Just follow me in this direction. I'm heading toward that bluff over there."

She stopped her wandering thoughts, managed a weak okay, and struggled on behind him, often stumbling over loose rocks as she continued up and up toward the bluff face now coming into view through the tree tops.

The faint trail grew fainter, more overgrown with weeds, and then vanished completely. Far ahead, his progress marked by the sound of dislodged rocks, Rob climbed.

Catherine, head down so she could watch her footing, chugged on and on.

Good grief, was she following today's version of Meriwether Lewis?

If she'd had the breath, she would have giggled at that idea. Did Rob expect to discover a new Missouri River over the next rise instead of the much smaller Buffalo River?

Catherine climbed for several more minutes before she realized she could no longer hear any sound—neither voice nor dislodged rocks—from Rob McCrite.

"Rob? Helloooo, Rob?"

Silence, except for her own breathing.

"Rob?"

Where was he?

Chapter 5

ROB TOOK HIS HAT off so he could look up more easily. How tall was the bluff? Must be two hundred and fifty feet...well, maybe at least two hundred. Not any sign that people had been here recently, not so much as a broken blade of grass.

Bluffshelters in this area reminded him of historic sites he'd explored in Arizona and New Mexico. The earliest people using the caves here could have been nomadic hunters, maybe the Paleo-Indians, like those who left evidence of their presence in Chaco Canyon, New Mexico, some 10,000 years ago.

A couple of thousand years later the Dalton people must have passed through here too. If so, they probably used the bluffshelters, though Dr. Fletcher said last winter that evidence of Dalton presence—their distinctive spear points and other tools—was almost nonexistent in the park. There were, however, at least a few documented Dalton pieces from this area in private collections. How many more had disappeared? That, Anderson Fletcher wouldn't speculate about. Dalton remnants found here would be valuable because of rarity if for no other reason.

The Archaic people who came next in history gradually settled in for longer periods and, by the end of their era and on into the time of the Woodland people, Buffalo River dwellers were diversifying into plant horticulture, scratching soil and scattering seeds from food-producing plants they'd gathered in the wild. Lots of possibilities for interesting discoveries dating from that time on, especially since groups remained here for larger parts of the year and, presumably, left behind more traces of their households and food-gathering activities. Could be all kinds of treasures still here for people like Anderson Fletcher—or Rob McCrite—to find. There might be pottery, which came into use during those centuries.

Rob moved closer to the bluff face and reached out to touch cold chert, realizing he was looking at raw material for tools. He scuffed his feet back and forth in the talus piled at the base of the sheer wall and saw no signs of stone chips that might indicate tool making.

Humans were always inventing things to make their lives easier. Pointed sticks to stone hoes to tractors with plows. Straw brooms to vacuums to vacuuming robots.

He laughed aloud as he pictured a robot lurching around the dusty floor of the Indian Rockhouse. He'd tell Catherine about that idea. She'd...

Catherine. What was keeping her? She should be here by now.

"Catherine? Catherine?"

Maybe she'd stopped in the bushes somewhere to get rid of morning coffee. Something like that. She'd be along soon.

He touched the bluff face again. The old ones had been here. He could almost feel their presence, their breath.

Rob began moving again, walking carefully through the slippery rock piles, eyeing them before and after each step.

He was mindful of safety, but, even more, of the possibility he would spot flakes left by stone tool makers.

After traveling several hundred feet, he saw what might be primitive stone steps rising from the valley floor. Man-made? Surely not. But weren't they too regular to be natural? Weathered. Broken rock in a zigzag pattern?

He felt heart thumps pulsing in his face and told himself to calm down. Logically he wasn't going to discover anything undiscovered here, but he was surely outside the boundaries of National Park land now, and for that reason might come upon something significant. Maybe.

He started climbing the bluff face, using the step-like rock surface when he could, carefully choosing hand holds and places to brace his feet when the steps vanished. He lost his footing several times, and—once—slid painfully almost to the bottom of the bluff. Increasing heart thumps reminded him that, even for someone used to exploration and climbing in rough places, this was a challenging undertaking. But he kept climbing.

A tangle of vines dropping from crevices near the top of the bluff almost stopped him. He wasn't sure they would hold his weight if he used them to pull farther up, and their twisting tendrils blocked safe access to firm rock. He clung to the bluff face for a few moments, assessing his situation. He'd seen no evidence of any prior human presence since leaving Catherine on the trail, and now he'd climbed within about thirty feet of the bluff top without seeing anything. Suddenly he felt like he'd been incredibly foolish. *But...only thirty feet or so more...*

Rob grabbed a vine, yanked. It held. Slowly, hand over hand, he pulled himself higher.

When he broke through the vines and saw the opening, he wanted to whoop with excitement and wondered if

Catherine was now close enough to hear him.

I really can have something important to show her when she catches up. She'll feel the fire of discovery, I know it. She's already recognized a life connection with ancient fossils, and yesterday she pretended to be an Indian Rockhouse dweller. She is so...smart, so...tuned in.

For a minute his heart thrilled at the possibilities for sharing this discovery with Catherine, and he considered waiting for her to reach the base of the bluff. Then the explorer's blood beating in his head pulled him forward. Logically, he wouldn't be the first person here in recent times, but the area looked so untouched.

Ignoring his precarious location far above ground level and the lack of secure footing, Rob left the relative safety of the vines and scrambled toward the dark opening. Just a few more feet and he would learn if he'd found something significant. *Oh, if only...*

He'd just pulled himself onto the cave floor and was lying spread-eagle catching his breath when he saw the shovel and pick lying a few inches from his fingertips.

At the same moment he sensed quick movement above his body and felt a sharp pain on the back of his head.

After that, Rob felt nothing at all.

Chapter 6

CATHERINE DECIDED to quit worrying about appearing weak and wimpish when she saw the flat, tree-shaded rock. She was tired, she was hot, and she was, by golly, going to sit. She settled down on the cool surface, took out her water bottle, sipped, and then shut her eyes, enjoying the solitude.

A puff of wind blew loose strands of sweat-damp hair against her cheek, so she took off her hat and tugged at her ponytail band, releasing the rest of her hair to swing free. As she enjoyed its weight moving in the breeze, she thought back to the Indian Rockhouse and wondered if Rob had noticed she might fit the description of someone named Autumn Moon. Her hair was long, a bit wavy, and dark brown—almost black. She usually wore it in a tight chignon, but of course a ponytail was more suitable for this camping trip. Her eyes were dark brown, her skin tawny. Both she and Henry had their father's coloring. Maybe Henry knew of Indian blood somewhere in the family.

Autumn Moon and Standing Bear.

The urge to meet bodily needs would have driven our lives eight or ten thousand years ago. Simple wants. Passions. Fulfill-

ment at the most basic level. A life less complicated.

Kill or be killed applied too. For that matter, it sometimes did today.

There would have been no books, no secure warmth or cooling, no steady food supply from the local grocery. Would story tellers have been enough for learning and entertainment, and an elder's wisdom acceptable as law?

She would never know. Technology, ages of learning, all the present knowledge that drove humankind could not be erased. No one could erase that silver Thunderbird. She couldn't be Autumn Moon, not even in her dreams. Life was so much more complicated now. No returning to basics.

She looked around the clearing. This was a great place to wait for Rob. He could explore the bluff all he wanted while she had her quiet time here. He'd find her when he came back for their lunch on the riverbank.

Peaceful. No sounds but bird calls and soft, friendly rustles caused by breezes and ground creatures scurrying about. White wildflowers growing in clusters at the base of the rock. Pretty things. But then wildflowers weren't ever ugly.

She'd almost bought that wildflower identification book in the visitor center near their campground. Too bad she didn't, since Rob had now marched off with his copy. The ability to learn about these delicate plants would have been worth the extra weight in her backpack. She stared at the little flowers for a minute, memorizing their looks until she could get back to Tyler Bend and the book.

Another breeze rushed through her clearing and the flowers bobbed impishly, making her grin. Ahhhhh, nothing to fracture peace. No human sounds, not even an airplane overhead. At this moment, in this place, maybe she *could* daydream about Autumn Moon and Standing Bear.

Of course she wasn't totally alone, even here. She

wouldn't want to be totally alone, and right now it would be nice to see beyond the clearing, maybe spot where Rob was, but the trees had enough leaves on them to mask all but the nearest landscape. The bluff he'd been heading for was visible only at the top, its striated, swirling wall looming above the trees like a miniature piece of the Grand Canyon. He was probably working his way along its base, exploring bits and pieces, happy, excited, focused, even passionate.

Oh, well, Catherine...right now second fiddle to archeology has to be good enough for you with Rob McCrite. At least the competition doesn't wear lipstick or have a soft, curvy body, not that he'd notice anything like that when there's exploring to be done.

When they kissed, she knew he realized she was a woman, but other than those short bursts of obvious feeling and attraction, he remained a remote puzzle. How the bubbly, enthusiastic, and somewhat unpredictable Carrie McCrite could produce this focused, intense son was part of that puzzle. He must be more like his father.

Whatever. It was a nice puzzle, and perhaps she could put the pieces together in the same way she organized cases for court. Learn. Assess. Prove. She would simply fit the Rob McCrite puzzle together in her mind and then—if she liked the picture that resulted—see if it fit into her life as well. Who knew...

The green curtain masking her distant view began to bounce and sway as another gust of wind shushed toward her. Once more she stared into the green, hoping to see a recognizable feature beyond it. The river must be in the valley below, but Rob had made so many turns while they were climbing that it was hard to judge where anything else might be. Except for the breeze-bounced leaves and a few midday bird calls, she heard no sound from Rob or anyone else.

"Well, now, hello there," a male voice said.

Catherine squeaked in surprise and jumped to her feet, turning toward the voice. He was still veiled in green as he approached from the direction of the bluff, and, embarrassed by her reaction to a simple greeting, she said, "Hello yourself," and sat on her rock again.

When he came into the clearing, the first thing she saw was the large knife hanging from his belt in its leather sheath. Was he hunting? Maybe he used that thing for skinning animals. Her entire body tensed as she fought to control a shudder.

He was very lean. The word *sinewy* popped into her head. Tall. Heavy, dark beard, curling. Hair straight, slicked back, a bit of grey. Weathered face, not bad-looking.

"Can I join you? I'd like to rest a minute."

She didn't know how she could say no, so she slid as far as possible toward one edge of the rock. "Sure, be my guest."

He sat, leaving only two or three inches between their bodies. "You alone?" he asked, looking around the clearing.

She stared at her lap and said, "I'm waiting for a friend." She wondered if he heard the shake in her voice, but then he should know that hideous knife might make anyone nervous.

When she lifted her head and saw him staring at the front of her shirt, shivery prickles of fear ran down her spine. His eyes looked odd. Drugs?

She rotated her shoulders to ease the building tension and, too late, realized he'd interpreted that as some kind of come-on gesture, since the rotation pushed her breasts more tightly against her shirt. His smile swerved into a leer.

Surely being frightened is silly, I'm imagining things. It's broad daylight, there are people around. There's Rob...

Imagination or not, it was time to get out of here. She stood, said, "Well, enjoy the rock, it's a pleasant place to rest. I've got to be going now and meet my friend."

"Thought you said you were waiting here for the friend."

"I...forgot, he's waiting for me in the parking lot." She backed two steps away.

He cocked his head to one side, seeming to think over what his next words would be. "Was this friend of yours a man wearing an orange shirt and khaki pants? Kinda reddish-brown hair?"

He'd described Rob. Now she had to get away, but shouldn't she run to find Rob first, be sure he was okay?

When he spoke again it was as if she'd affirmed his description aloud. "Your friend is exploring. He's forgotten about you, so I've got you to myself."

"What? I don't understand." *She hoped she was wrong about the imaginings stabbing through her thoughts like icicles.*

"You know you're on private land? You aren't in the park now."

"No, I..."

He got to his feet. Instinctively she took two more steps back and then turned to run, but his own steps were too fast. She yelped as his hand closed like a vise, twisting the flesh on her upper arm.

"Hold it there, we're gonna talk. What's your name?"

She said nothing, staring at the ground and thinking, oddly, of telling him her name was Autumn Moon.

"Now, now, be friendly with me." His hand dug deeply into her upper arm. "I'm not a bad sort, let's just get to know each other better, then maybe we can have us a party. Seein' you like this puts me in the mood for a party, how about you? Wouldn't you like a party? Other gals have.

"Come on you, talk to me." His hold tightened. A surge

of tears washed down her cheeks and she snuffled, coughed, spit snot. He laughed and jerked sideways to avoid the missile, then twisted her around, pulled her back against his chest, and ran his hand heavily over the front of her shirt. "Oh, yes, we're gonna have fun."

She could tell he was reacting strongly to her physical presence and suddenly felt she'd fallen out of her real self and dropped into a nightmare. A combination of rage and terror began burning through her and she jerked involuntarily, which brought a still tighter hold on her arm.

This isn't really happening. It's what you read about, it happens someplace else. It's noon, broad daylight for goodness' sake. If only Rob would come back.

The man had done nothing to conceal his face. She could identify him easily. How did he dare...

"Let me *go*. This is insane. There are people on the river. I'll scream."

Now he turned her to face him again, his fingers digging into her arm like clamps.

"Go ahead and holler all you want. You think anyone will hear? Naaa, not where we are, not here outside the park. You're gonna come with me and you're gonna keep your mouth shut." His voice dropped to a purr. "We're gonna have us a fine time together. I'll show you what a real man can do, and then maybe I'll let you go...after."

He looked at the watch on his free arm. "You're gonna have to wait, though. There's some urgent business I've gotta take care of first. Can't be helped, much as I'd like to play with you right now." He laughed, and sounded almost normal, happy. "So I'm gonna put you in storage, ready for me. And don't you forget, I'm the one who's got the big knife."

He laughed again as he began pulling her toward the bluff face.

All her ability for logical thought dropped into a white-out whirl of panic, and, conscious only of that panic, she stumbled along beside him for several minutes. Then, way back in her head, she realized she had to defeat the panic and think—think clearly. Her life probably depended on what she thought from now on.

Rape? Oh, dear God, whoever, wherever you are, please help me. Those rocks, hard to walk...arm hurts. What should I do? Try to get away? They say it's better to get away early because what happens after is going to be much worse...they say...but his hand is so strong, hurting...can't think what to do...oh...I can fall! That'll break his grip and then I'll run.

She bent her knees and started to drop, but he yanked her up before she got near the ground and, holding her firmly against his side, moved forward even more quickly, forcing her to stumble along with him—on, and on, and on.

Finally they broke out of a stand of river cane into a cleared area. A small square house stood at some distance across the clearing, but the man ignored it and pulled Catherine toward what looked like a garage built against the side of a bluff. He pushed the side door open, tugged her across a dirt floor, opened another door at the back and shoved her through it. She fell into dust and rocks—on the floor of a cave.

She lifted her head out of the dust and through the curtain of her hair saw boxes, tools, rope, even a wood chair with no back. He sat on her legs, throwing her backpack aside. His weight shifted as he reached into one of the boxes and took out something that rattled. She understood what it was when he pulled her hands behind her, twisting her shoulders painfully, and clicked metal handcuffs on her wrists. Why would he have handcuffs? Did he handcuff women before he...?

When he lifted his weight off her body, she tried to kick him but he grabbed her ankles and tied them together with rope, pulling her shoes off first.

"There now, you won't cause me any trouble," he said as he lifted her into sitting position and propped her against a rock. Then he moved away to light a lantern.

Am I going to die here—bloody, defiled? Oh, Rob.

He opened her backpack and inspected the sandwich and water bottle. "Lunch? Well, I'll let you eat later. Want you full of energy." Once more, there was the ugly laugh.

He took the knife out of its sheath, and before she could even begin to imagine being stabbed to death, he proceeded, in fast slices and rips, to shred and remove every scrap of her clothing. When he was slicing through her underpants his knife caught in the elastic, causing the point to twist downward and cut into her flesh. She stared at the scratch and counted drops of blood that welled up along the path of the blade. *This can't be happening...that's not real blood.*

When all she'd had covering her body was tossed on the cave floor, he looked over every bare inch, occasionally licking his lips. She was sure he drooled, but her mind, hot with shame and panic, might have imagined it.

After he'd had enough looking, he touched. She shut her eyes and willed her mind to quit processing what was happening. She gagged and wanted to vomit, but her stomach felt empty and dry retching would simply weaken her rather than repel him. She began shaking violently, her body now out of control.

"Cold? Well, we'll put you in a blanket."

She opened her eyes when she felt the wiry wool against her skin. It was red, its color dust-dulled.

He stood, put on a hat with a light, and then lifted her, grunting a bit as he lurched farther into the cave.

I can throw him off balance, make him fall. She squirmed, jerking her body back and forth wildly. He almost did fall before he regained balance, dropped her to her feet, and hit her across the face so hard that it felt like her neck had snapped. She tasted blood.

"You—stop it," he said, "or I'll do much worse."

Catherine went limp as he lifted her again, but she kept her eyes open, surveying her surroundings, and saw a side tunnel branching off the one they were in. Maybe, when he was gone, she could hide there. It might even lead to daylight.

Then the main tunnel changed. She noticed remnants of wood bracing, unnatural cuts through rock and, in one place, a partial cave-in. They must have passed into a mine shaft!

"Here we are."

He put her down by a large metal tank. Its top was jammed against a beam spanning the mine tunnel ceiling.

He pushed against the tank, moving it slightly. Dust and rocks showered all around them. The dust smelled old, like a closed-up house, vacant for many years. She sneezed, snuffled and coughed, then spit into the dust, raising a tiny cloud.

"You can get to your hanky in a minute, but now you look up here. See what this old boiler is doing? It's holding that beam. If it falls over, the ceiling comes down. I'm gonna cuff you to a pipe fastened on the boiler. If you wiggle too much—well, you see what'll happen, don't you?" He pushed at the tank again and more dirt and rock fell.

"Best be very still while you wait for me, I won't be long." He laughed. "I hope you're not afraid of the dark."

He unwrapped the blanket, then took a key chain from his pocket, opened the handcuff on her right wrist, re-

snapped it around the boiler pipe. He didn't bother to put
the blanket back over her, but she was sitting on it and at
least it offered some protection from the rocks.

He looked at his watch again and, hurrying now, cut the
rope binding her ankles, leaving only one wrist fastened to
the pipe. "There, you're free enough if you want to pee or
eat your lunch." He tossed the backpack into her lap. "But
don't forget, you move the boiler just a little bit, the whole
shebang comes down on you."

He fell silent. She was sure his eyes were on her body
again, but the headlamp's glare blocked her vision. All she
could see was a dark outline against the mine tunnel wall.
If he touched her now she *would* scream, and he could just
kill her on the spot. *No, no, I didn't mean that, I...* Out-of-
control tears began flowing down her cheeks.

She saw him move and braced herself for whatever
might be coming, but he turned and hurried away down the
tunnel, leaving her in the most intense darkness she'd ever
known.

Chapter 7

CARRIE CAME BACK TO earth when the book on her lap began a slide toward the floor. As she caught it, she realized she'd been floating in a day dream, trying—with minimum success—to picture Henry standing on a mysterious riverbank holding a fishing pole. He said yesterday he'd caught several fish but they were all too small to keep, so hot dogs and canned chili were on the supper menu for himself and the kids. "Maybe there'll be fish for the three of us tomorrow night," he told her.

That would be tonight now. Was he catching a big fish right this minute? Again she tried to picture Henry fishing, and wondered how one changed live fish from the river into fish for frying. Ugh. It couldn't be pleasant.

The image of a long-ago dead fish came at her without warning. That fish stared up from a dinner plate with one glazed eye. Not wanting to shame Amos McCrite at a bar association banquet where he was being honored, she ate her baked potato first, pushed its skin over the poor fish's head, then ate a few bites from the section between the silvery tail and shrouded eye. It had been hard going, but when she thought of it as simply part of her job as Amos's wife, it wasn't so bad.

She'd taken the wife job with her own eyes wide open. At nearly thirty she still lived with her parents and wanted a home of her own. Amos, rising rapidly in his law career, wanted a presentable hostess and wife standing beside him at public events.

They'd met at the library where she worked. He requested a research assistant. She helped him locate old newspaper files. Even after his work with the newspapers was finished, she often saw him in the library, and he seemed to be watching her. By the time he asked her to dinner, she'd begun to feel edgy about his attention. If she hadn't known he was a reputable criminal lawyer, she'd probably have turned him down.

When Amos McCrite proposed to her, he pulled no punches about what he expected from a wife.

She accepted anyway.

Carrie figured he admired her accommodating attitude and quiet knowledge when she assisted library patrons, and she'd tried to conduct her job as his wife in the same way. For whatever reason, it worked.

The fact the two of them managed to produce Rob was still her own form of miracle. They had rarely touched, let alone do anything more intimate. Amos certainly wouldn't have been bumping into her at the kitchen sink like Henry did. Amos never said...couldn't say he loved her, either.

Fishing. Would Henry cut fish heads and tails off at the river? Then what? The whole scene was difficult to visualize.

On the other hand, she could visualize Henry himself very easily. By now she was familiar with almost every inch of his body, and...

Stop thinking about Henry.

Carrie looked at the clock on the table beside her: 8:00.

No wonder she was hungry. She wondered if Eleanor and
Jason would like to go into town for breakfast at the Ice
House Coffee Shop. They probably hadn't eaten yet. Maybe
Shirley could join them. She'd said yesterday that Roger and
Junior would be leaving early this morning for a cattle sale.

A "Yowp" came from Henry's chair, and she looked over
to see FatCat unroll long legs and lean body, stretch, and
yawn. Then the cat sat on her haunches and surveyed Carrie
with reproachful blue eyes.

Carrie stared back. *Silly! Reproach? Pure imagination. Just
because Henry spoils her...*

The cool blue glare continued.

"Oh, come on then," Carrie said, patting her lap.

FatCat stayed where she was.

"Have it your way." Odd, how loud her voice sounded
in the quiet house.

She went back to thinking about Henry. He'd said
yesterday that the kids were exploring a ghost town in the
morning and planned to go canoeing in the afternoon. Then
he mentioned casually that Rob and Catherine had two very
nice-looking tents. She'd nodded to herself with satisfaction,
but he couldn't see that of course, and she didn't comment.
She merely said, "Ghost town?"

"On the river below here, an old zinc mining town
named Rush. I gather it was a boom town beginning more
than a hundred years ago. The mines faded out after World
War I, and the town was pretty much gone after World War
II. I'm sure they'll tell me all about it when they come back."

He paused, then said, "Cara, I sure miss you. I guess you
and FatCat are enjoying your girls-only week?"

He didn't leave time for her response before he hurried
on, and it occurred to Carrie he might be afraid of hearing
the answer to his question.

"So, what's been happening there since you finished cleaning and re-organizing our kitchen? Are the Stacks and Booths doing anything interesting?"

She'd searched through her head for news. "Well, Roger's going to a cattle sale tomorrow. I gather he wants to find a new bull for his girls. Fresh genes in the herd. Nothing else different since you left day before yesterday." She'd laughed and reminded him, "It's only been two days."

"And a night," he said, "so it seems longer."

The man was an incurable romantic. "I know, Henry love. I miss you, and FatCat does too, but see how much you're enjoying fishing and getting to know Rob and Catherine better? I'd just be in the way."

"Like heck," he'd said, and after a final, "I love you," hung up.

Okay, time to think about breakfast. She punched in Shirley's number.

"I'd sure like to go with you," Shirley said, "but I already ate plenty with Roger and Junior. Have you heard from Henry?"

"He's been fishing, but the fish he caught were too small to keep."

"Happens. You might tell him he's welcome to fish in our creek whenever he likes. Just give us a call first. Roger and I catch pretty good trout out back of here. We didn't know Henry was a fisherman, or we'd have asked him to come down before."

"I didn't know he liked to fish, either. But he does, so that's that."

"You ever fish?"

Carrie laughed. "Hardly! Mom and Dad weren't outdoor people, and I believe Amos thought fish could only be created by chefs, drowned in fancy sauce, sprinkled with al-

monds, and put before him by an attentive person who said
Sir a lot. I'd never seen a fishing pole up close until Henry
showed me his."

She hesitated a moment before she decided to go on
with her confession. "I have been looking at raw fish in the
grocery and wondering how people cook it. I like fish, but
I've always eaten it in restaurants or brought it home already
prepared and frozen. If there's a chance Henry's going to
come back with raw fish, I guess I should get a cookbook
about fixing it. He hasn't said anything about his plans,
though, and now I wonder... Well, I wouldn't mind cooking
it so much if it didn't really look like a fish. You know what
I mean?"

"I reckon I do. Land, woman, fish is one of the easiest
things to get ready, that is if someone else cleans and fillets
it first. The person who catches it most always does that and
I'm sure Henry would. He probably hasn't said anything
because he has no idea what he'll catch or be able to keep."

After a second's pause, Shirley's usually calm voice
picked up a fleck of excitement. "My gracious, I have fish
in our freezer. Why don't you come down here tomorrow
afternoon for a cooking lesson? Then you can stay for supper
and we'll eat the fish you cooked."

"I wouldn't want to..."

"Hush now. Be here by four o'clock. Why don't you
bring some of your raspberry-cranberry salad? Go good with
fish. Roger likes that and so do I. We'll see if Junior can
figure out what's in it. For a thirty-eight-year-old man, he's
pretty smart about food.

"Well, now, you enjoy your breakfast, and be sure and
tell Henry hello from us if he calls. Don't let on about coming here for cooking fish, though. You can surprise him after
he gets home, and I'll bet you're right eager for that time to

come."

Carrie, lost in thought, let the silence go on so long that
Shirley said, "Aren't you now?"

"Yes," Carrie said finally, "yes. I am."

She ended up going to breakfast alone, because Eleanor and
Jason were just heading out the door to attend a gift fair
in Fayetteville when she phoned them. Jason now seemed
as caught up in planning for *Eleanor's Flower Garden* as his
wife was. Though Shirley and Carrie helped Eleanor gather
ideas—and merchandise—for her flower and garden shop
initially, Jason had recently replaced them as Eleanor's partner on most buying trips. "I'm buying lots of stuff now, and
someone has to carry the boxes and do my bookkeeping,"
Eleanor explained.

Carrie missed the shopping and planning with her
friends, but she and Shirley agreed they were glad Jason was
involved instead. He had been rather at loose ends since
turning over his manufacturing business in Ohio to their
son Tom. On the other hand Eleanor, a quiet housewife
in her previous life, leaped into new strength after Jason's
retirement and their move south.

"She's a better woman now, mostly because she's been
part of some of your adventures to help people," Shirley had
once said to Carrie, "especially that time when she had to
fight to save her own life.[1] I don't mean it's right she should
have to do that exactly, but things came out okay, and in
the end it was good for her. She sure got new respect from
Jason. He's learned she can do more than cook and clean
house. A husband needs to know that, I think.

"Roger now, he's always known it, since I've worked
beside him on the farm from the beginning. Had one of my

---

[1] *A Treasure to Die For*

babies in the milking barn for a fact. I reckon that proved how devoted I am to my job!"

Carrie had listened and laughed while Shirley related the story of the birth in the barn with Roger and ten cows assisting. *How lucky I am to have such good—and very different—friends,* she thought.

"The Triumvirate," Henry called them, and he wasn't far from being right.

Once she knew she'd be eating alone, Carrie decided to grab a breakfast sandwich at the Sonic and go visit former co-workers in the Arkansas Tourist Information Center north of Bonnie. The staff had changed some in the months since she'd left her job there, but she enjoyed swapping tourist stories whether those on duty were long-time employees or new ones.

Carrie was halfway to the drive-in before she realized she'd left her cell phone at home. Henry wanted her to carry it with her in the car in case she had a flat tire or some other problem. She started to turn around, but then thought, *Oh, never mind, it's not worth going all the way back. The car's fine, I have new tires, and Henry won't be calling again until at least four o'clock. Besides, I got along without a cell phone for years.*

So she forgot about the phone and drove on.

Chapter 8

HENRY THOUGHT ABOUT cigarettes. Imagined tapping one out of the pack to slide between his fingers—lighting it—knew the taste too well. Smoke drifting like a sigh.

Nuts. Haven't smoked in twenty years, won't ever again. Just nerves...blast it all, where are the kids?

He shifted in the lawn chair where he'd been waiting for first light. He'd come awake before five, not knowing if worry returned with waking or had been part of a dream. He left his sleeping bag, dressed, stepped out into the coolness, started his propane stove, made instant coffee, and sat listening to the river.

Stupid. They were adults, not children one had to wait up for, though he had waited up until midnight. Then he'd convinced himself such concern about two capable adults was crazy and crawled in his sleeping bag. Long years in law enforcement taught him how to put worry in a category unrelated to sleep and he did fall asleep quickly, but then awakened, worrying. Wished he could talk with Carrie, but wouldn't call her, not yet at least. From her distance it would be a huge worry. All the what-ifs got worse if you weren't on the scene.

He heard a car motor start, warm, drop into idle. Sounded like it was coming from over by the kids' camping area. He stared that way, already knowing it couldn't be Catherine's Jeep, not that engine—too smooth. The motor speeded up, racing as the driver gunned it in short bursts. He was impatient about something.

Has to be a he, and I'd bet his sleepy neighbors could throttle him, Henry thought, chuckling at his own little joke. *Here's a man in love with his wheels. Probably thinks you should be honored if his car's engine noise wakes you up.*

But Henry couldn't remember seeing any vehicle out of the ordinary in the campground last night. Mostly trucks, SUV's, vans. So, an early visitor? Very early.

He heard the car back onto the campground road and start toward him. *Whoo-ee, yes, vintage Thunderbird, probably '57, silver paint gleaming in the new light. Man driving. Now that's a car I'd like to drive myself...just once.*

Henry watched the Thunderbird disappear up the road, then went back to thinking about the kids.

Maybe it wasn't so odd Rob and Catherine hadn't come back for hot dogs and chili last night. Canned chili and hot dogs with him weren't exactly glamorous, even when enjoyed by a campfire. Lots more interesting things they could have been eating. Been doing. Gone clear to Harrison for a fancy meal, slept in a motel. Rented a canoe, decided to spend the night on a gravel bar. Did they take their sleeping bags with them? Maybe they'd hiked until dark and stayed overnight in a cabin near Rush. Whatever. No requirement to tell him. Might even resent his concern.

But his thoughts wouldn't stop ricocheting between worry and anger. They should have told him, he was family, he cared about them. Even though they were adults, they could have said something like, "We might camp out overnight on a gravel bar, we might drive to Harrison. We... might..." whatever.

They could have said, "Don't worry, Henry."

It wasn't like Rob. He'd have used his cell phone, called. He wouldn't simply disappear with no word. Well, maybe he would. Maybe he and Catherine wanted privacy.

But to disappear with no word?

Enough light to see by now. He got up from the lawn chair, started down the campground road. It had been eight hours since his last walk-around, and he sure hoped he was going to see a red Jeep at their camp site.

No red Jeep. Camp site quiet. Dead quiet. Two tents zipped shut. He decided to look inside at least one of them. Maybe stuff would be gone, enough stuff to make camping out overnight workable. Guy in the space next door had just come out of his RV with a coffee cup in his hand. He looked Henry over, started to walk toward him. Walked very slowly. An implied menace in his attitude. Big guy. Didn't shave when he was on vacation.

"Did you see these two come back?" Henry asked. "I wondered if they'd come back during the night."

"Nope." The guy stopped, just stood there. T-shirt. Cut-offs.

"I was going to check inside their tents, see if they took sleeping bags and decided to sleep along the river."

"Oh?" The word was heavy, drawn out.

He ignored the man. After all, he had every right to look inside their tents. They were family. He was worried about them, not planning to steal their stuff. Henry wished he could just pull out his old Kansas City police shield and say, "It's okay, I'm a cop." Instead he said, "The three of us are family." Any more explanation was unnecessary.

He knelt by the first tent, ran the zipper on the flap, looked inside. There was a neatly rolled sleeping bag at the back. Shaving gear. Rob's tent.

"Maybe they went to a motel last night."

"Yeah?" The man in cut-offs wasn't moving.

Henry closed the flap, got to his feet, said, "Well, have a nice day," and then cringed at the stupid remark. He began walking, face ahead, until he reached the campground road and had turned toward his own site. Only then did he look back. Rob and Catherine's neighbor was at the door of his RV, eyes still on Henry. Like he was guarding their stuff. Okay, that was good.

With each step along the quiet road it became increasingly difficult to keep his thoughts from bouncing over multiple possibilities, again and again and again. Maybe they had car trouble. Maybe...

He sat in his lawn chair. What time did the ranger come on duty at Tyler Bend? He hoped it would be the same one as yesterday. An okay guy. Name tag said Shane Lind as he recalled. Comfortable to talk with. He'd understand. Didn't seem the type to assume Henry was overreacting. He'd know what should be done—if anything.

Shane. Henry remembered the old movie, Shane, and wondered if this man's mother and dad had seen it before their son was born.

He reached in his food box for a breakfast bar and a can of juice, dumped more coffee crystals in his cup, poured water. As soon as he finished eating, he'd walk up to the visitor center and wait on a bench there until someone came. Watch the road for a red Jeep.

The sign said the center opened at 8:30 A.M. until Memorial Day, 8:00 through the summer, but it was only 7:45 when

Ranger Shane Lind drove into the employee parking lot. Henry got to his feet and was peering through the door glass when office lights went on and, eventually, Lind showed up at the counter carrying a stack of papers. Henry, too worried now to be polite, banged on the glass.

A quick glance from the man, papers dropped on the counter, a hurried walk to open the door. *Maybe,* Henry thought, *I look as worried as I feel.*

Years in the police department had taught him how to make a concise report, and before five minutes had passed, Ranger Lind was on the phone to the Buffalo Point Ranger Station. After a few words he handed the phone to Henry.

Yes, red Jeep Cherokee. Didn't know what year, fairly new. Oklahoma license plate. No, he didn't know the number.

"The fee collector can get a license number off their registration," the voice on the phone said. "Did they have a trailer, a canoe rack—anything like that?"

No, nothing like that, and Henry hadn't a clue what Catherine might have stored inside the Cherokee that would be visible through windows.

He could give a physical description of Rob and Catherine, knew their ages, remembered something about their backpacks, but had no idea what they were wearing yesterday. He'd been on the river fishing before they got up.

After the ranger on duty at Buffalo Point said he had no more questions for Henry at the moment, Ranger Lind began calling canoe concessionaires to ask if any of them rented a canoe to Rob McCrite or Catherine King yesterday.

Henry waited, strolled around the small museum in the center, looked, saw nothing.

Before forty-five minutes had passed, they knew the worst. A locked red Jeep was parked in the Rush lot. There was no evidence of Rob or Catherine anywhere in the immediate area. No canoe agencies had rented to them and no canoes were unaccounted for.

"Now what?" Henry asked.

"Come back here in the office, have a seat, and tell me more about this couple," Lind said.

Henry moved behind the counter, sat, struggled to reach beyond anxiety toward sensible responses.

"You said they each have a cell phone?"

"Yes, and neither of them called to say they wouldn't be back. They said nothing at supper the evening before about not returning to the campground last night."

He realized he'd just repeated something he said earlier, but after all this wasn't a police report, this was personal. That personal part gave him an excuse for a few peculiarities.

"Tell me all you know about their plans for yesterday, and more about their specific interests here." The ranger's voice was smooth, calm. "For example," he continued, "the mines at Rush are off limits, but might they have tried to enter one? Are they climbers? One of them could have gotten stuck in a mine or cave, or fallen during a climb."

"If that happened, wouldn't the other have called for help...called me? Shane...oh, sorry, Ranger Lind."

"Shane is fine."

"They're both responsible people, Shane, almost stuffy if you know what I mean. Rob's a college professor, Catherine's a lawyer. Proper to the core. I can't see either of them taking foolish chances."

Well, maybe that was a slight exaggeration. It all depended, didn't it, especially with Rob? Under some circumstances...

Henry rested his elbows on his knees, leaned forward, looked at the floor, didn't know what more to say.

The ranger filled the silence, thinking aloud. "It is odd one of them hasn't gotten in touch, no matter what happened. There are places in the park where cell phones don't receive well, but usually a person can walk to a clear location and call for help."

He hesitated, and then asked, "Is there anything more you can think of that might assist us in the search?"

Henry considered this, decided to say what he'd been thinking. "Rob was excited about this trip. His field is American Indian History, and he's strongly interested in archeology. He talked with your staff archeologist last winter, and I think his interest along that line is one reason he came here. I suppose it's possible he went into a cave—maybe wasn't cautious because he thought he'd found something, and...what? Got stuck? Fell? But Catherine is not a caver and is not foolhardy. I don't think...well, I just don't know..."

"You say Catherine King is your sister?"

"Half-sister, and half my age. Rob is my wife's son by her former marriage. The two of them met at our wedding and...well, you don't need to know all that." As an afterthought he said, more to himself than to the ranger, "I think Catherine just came on the trip to be with Rob, though she does enjoy physical activity and the outdoors."

Shane Lind got to his feet, hesitated a moment, then briefly rested his hand on Henry's shoulder. "We'll find them, Henry, we always do. We're beginning the search at Rush now, since their car is in the lot there."

"I'm a retired police officer with some experience in searches, at least in a city landscape. I'd like to help. Just tell me what I can do."

"You'll help most by staying here. You don't know the area around Rush, and it can be quite rugged, even dangerous. We don't want to lose you, too. Besides, they might come back at any time. You should watch for their return and be where we can reach you easily."

Henry shook his head, started to protest, then thought better of it and said nothing. He was on their turf.

But surely anyone on the staff here would react immediately if they saw a red Jeep Cherokee; they didn't need him to watch for that. As for finding him easily, they had his cell phone number, didn't they?

"Our rangers are skilled at search and rescue. We lose someone every so often and we always find them. I know waiting is going to be tough, and I can't stop you from driving to Rush like any tourist, but you shouldn't get involved. My advice is to stay here.

"Meanwhile, is there anyone you want to notify?"

Henry couldn't put off calling Carrie any longer. For one thing, she'd begin praying for Rob and Catherine. That might help keep her from panicking. And it would probably help him, too.

But how was he going to handle telling her?

Dear God, what am I going to say?

Chapter 9

HOT. *BRIGHT LIGHT HURT.* His fingers curled, felt dust. Then Rob McCrite went back to feeling nothing.

After an unknown time he opened his eyes again. The sun had shifted, leaving the bluffshelter in shadow. He lifted his head. *Ow, not a good idea.* Keeping his head close to the dust, he belly-crawled, one short wiggle after another, toward the nearest cave wall and turned in a quarter-circle until he was lying on his side with his back against the wall. Moving an inch at a time, waiting for dizziness to pass between each move, he pushed into a sitting position and looked at his surroundings as carefully as a head full of fuzz and a raging headache would allow. More time passed.

Gotta think. Where is this? There's a cave opening back there. I'm high above the ground, can see tree tops in the distance. But, how did I get up here?

He moved his fingers toward the pain coming from the back of his head. There was a bump centered between his ears as well as something crusty. Dried blood?

Climbing...someone hit me...can't remember...

He had seen a pick and a shovel, hadn't he? Yes, over there. The shovel was gone, but the pick—he could still see the pick. He hadn't been hallucinating.

Thirsty. Where was his backpack? Gone too, with his water bottle and cell phone.

He turned his head to study a flat sheet of rock lying in the center of the shelter floor. Must have dropped from the ceiling eons ago. The rock looked like a piece from a giant puzzle. He considered this, processing the puzzle rock through an educated memory that, thank goodness, hadn't dissolved in fuzz. Maybe the New Madrid quakes along the Mississippi in 1811 and 1812 jolted the rock loose. And maybe not. For all he knew it came down last week. He was no geologist, and in this dry dust, couldn't guess a time.

The fallen piece had cracked near the center, with chunks of it lying in dust on either side of the crack. Did the pick make those chunks? Was someone breaking the rock up to see what could be hidden underneath?

After a few minutes Rob slid down the wall, rolled on his stomach again, and began pushing forward, this time toward the bluffshelter opening. Dizziness overwhelmed him when he tried to lift his head and look down. *Whoa.* He tried again, and this time handled the dizziness long enough to hang his head over the edge and manage a look. Whoops, nausea.

Way down there, is that a man lying on the ground? Hard to focus. Too dizzy.

Rob scooted back, put his head down, groaned.

At least it isn't a woman lying there.

Woman? Why did he think it might be a woman...?

Catherine? Catherine. No! No!

Catherine finished saying all the swear words she could think of for the second time and started around again. After the third run-through she laughed, and in her ears it sounded like a child's wail. "Mom, oh, Mom, I'm sorry. You can yell at me all you want. Oh, Mom..."

I'm hysterical. This won't do.

She shifted on the blanket, which bounced the backpack in her lap. Backpack! The monster hadn't looked beyond the sandwich. He hadn't searched her backpack.

Her shaking hand finally defeated the Velcro fastening and she dug inside, found her windbreaker, and shrugged her free arm into it, pulling the other side over her shoulder. The jacket only came to her waist, but even that much cover comforted her.

Once the jacket was on she felt in the backpack again. *They were here! Her cell phone and her wind-up flashlight.* For the first time she was glad the monster hadn't thought beyond sex. *What an idiot, he'd left her cell phone.*

But of course she was the idiot. A quick click told her the cell phone wouldn't work in here. The flashlight did, but it had to be cranked, not so easy when one hand was fastened to a pipe. Adjusting to her situation, Catherine worked at cranking smoothly, and, finally getting the hang of it, turned the handle around and around until she figured she had given herself—according to the advertising blurb she remembered from the L.L.Bean catalogue—about an hour of light.

The light told her nothing new about her prison. Still the same huge boiler jammed against the ceiling, the same crumbling walls. She was imprisoned in the earth as surely as if she'd been buried alive. And the monster might come back to her prison any minute. Then...

Hysteria threatened once more and she went back to cranking around and around, as fast as she could.

Henry paced the paths near the visitor center, dialing his

home phone, then Carrie's cell phone, over and over. He got only the answering machine at home, nothing at all on her cell phone. Where was she?

Finally he sat on the nearest bench, trying to organize his tumbling thoughts. Sort things out. Should he even be calling Carrie? She'd be alone. Such news as he had wasn't something he wanted her to face alone. *What could he do?*

Maybe it was just as well he hadn't reached her. It would be best to call Shirley or Eleanor first so someone would be with her.

Shirley. She'd be the one to help them. So sensible, and so...motherly. He punched in Shirley's number, and, thank goodness, she answered after two rings.

"Missing? Oh, my. Did you...did they...? Well, I reckon by now you've about done all the things I'd think of, haven't you?

"I don't know where Carrie is. She phoned a couple of hours ago, wanted me to go to breakfast with her at the Ice House Coffee Shop, but I'd eaten. Maybe she went there with Eleanor. Let me check around and you phone me back in about thirty minutes.

"Don't worry, I'll chase her down. She can call you and you can tell her...but I wonder now, shouldn't we maybe think about coming there? I know I can't keep her here after she finds out her son is missing. Let's see, I can leave a note for Roger and Junior if they don't get home in time, and then drive us there. How long did it take you to make it? Three hours? No, don't fuss, Henry, I need to do this. We all do for each other, you know that.

"Can you get us a place to stay near where you are—a cabin, or something like it? Something with a kitchen would be nice. We can buy groceries along the way; I want to leave what I have here for Roger and Junior in case I'm gone for more'n a day.

"You go on, get busy now. Find us a place while I'm looking for Carrie. If I can't find her, I'll leave a message to call me as soon as she comes in. You didn't say anything on your machine, did you? Good, best to tell her in person. I'll let you know what I've found out when you phone me back."

Henry ended the call with a sigh of relief and headed toward the campground to get his truck. He'd try at Buffalo River Outfitters for a cabin. They were just outside the entrance to Tyler Bend.

He hesitated but then veered toward the visitor center. Maybe he should check in with Shane first, tell him the plans, and see if there was any news from the searchers.

Carrie went to the kitchen as soon as she came in the house. She'd stayed away longer than intended, but her good friend Sarah Simmons was on duty at the tourist center today, and they had a lot of catching up to do. Only hunger finally ended their chatter, sending Sarah to her lunch box and Carrie to her car.

She made a peanut butter and jelly sandwich and, while chewing, listened to the message on her answering machine.

"It's Shirley. Can I come up? Ring me back."

Thirty minutes later Carrie put the phone down after her call to Henry and sat staring at Shirley. "He said missing. How can that be? I know it's a big park, but how can two sensible adults simply be missing?" She sat in silence for a minute, then jumped to her feet. "I've got to go there, help look for them. Surely there's something no one has thought of. I need to see the place...I need..."

"I was pretty sure you'd say that. Why don't I drive us? I'll go home, get my things together, and be back as soon as

I can. You get your stuff ready now. Henry has us a place to stay, a log cabin with a kitchen, so we'll stop for groceries in Harrison."

Carrie started to say, "I can drive myself," but then stopped, realizing Shirley's offer was a Godsend. She wasn't sure she could face making that long drive alone.

Instead of her half-formed protest, she said, "FatCat..."

"Don't you worry about FatCat. The guys will see to her. Go on now, get your stuff. Don't forget jeans and hiking shoes, and it might get chilly along the river at night so be sure you have a jacket." With that motherly advice and a quick hug, Shirley was gone.

After sitting quietly for a few moments Carrie went to the phone and dialed the number of a woman from her church. A brief explanation of what was happening brought the promise of support in prayer. Feeling somewhat comforted, she put the phone down and went to pack for her trip to the Buffalo National River.

Chapter 10

ROB'S MIND CRAWLED back to awareness when beams of sunlight found their way inside the shelter. He sat up and wiped his hand across his face, an unconscious gesture aimed at organizing his thoughts. He had fallen asleep some time during the dark hours after all.

Degrees of dark and light. That was the only way he could identify time. His watch was gone. The missing watch, once of much more value than a plastic bottle full of water, was now unimportant. He'd trade it for a drink of water in a second. Funny about priorities.

He slid to the rim of the bluffshelter and looked over the edge. The man was still down there. Was he the thief, the one who had taken the watch and backpack? Rob wondered, bizarrely, if his watch had been broken when the man fell.

He studied the landscape below him more carefully. Didn't seem the ground was getting any closer to his level. He started a chuckle, thinking about the possibility of land rising up to meet him, then stopped, gasping. Laughing did something painful inside his head. Still, the throbbing just above the nape of his neck had calmed a lot since yesterday. Unless he laughed.

Anyway, the ground down there wasn't about to get any closer, so if Catherine didn't come with help soon, he'd have to try a descent on his own. But...how had he ever made it up here? Those first four or five yards below the opening appeared to be without foot- or handholds, and there was nothing to break a fall once it began. The dead man was proof enough of that.

Going down looked impossible, especially in his present state, but if help didn't come before he got too weak, he'd have to try it. There were no other options.

He turned his head to study a tangle of vines dropping down the bluff face. The nearest cluster was over three yards away. He couldn't reach it, even assuming it had the strength to hold him.

Once more he looked at the cave opening in the back wall of the shelter. That avenue was closed without a flashlight. If he'd heard water running in the cave, he might have risked a few minutes of exploration, feeling his way in the dark, but caves here were notoriously dry, and cool air currents from this one smelled of dust, not dampness.

The very thought of going over the edge to begin a climb down made him shiver. But, could he last without water until help came?

Why hadn't Catherine come yesterday? She'd been just behind him as they hiked through the woods, and she knew his destination. Surely she would have been concerned when he didn't return at noon. So, why hadn't she come? Why hadn't he heard her calling, *"Rob, Rob?"*

Then it struck him that Catherine might have been here while he was unconscious, called his name, and when he didn't respond, went looking somewhere else.

But wouldn't she have returned here when she didn't find him? And wouldn't she have seen that dead man on the ground?

He must be dead. There had been no sign of life all this
time.

If Catherine or someone else came, they'd have noticed
the man, would have looked up...

This was definitely weird. By now people should be bus-
tling about below, investigating what had happened to the
man, looking to see where he'd fallen from.

Rob shuddered again. It was also possible the man had
fallen during his climb up or down and not directly from
the shelter.

If help had arrived quickly, would it have made a differ-
ence to that man—whether he lived or died?

How, and when, did he fall?

The picture Rob couldn't get out of his head was that
he, Rob McCrite, might have pushed the man over the
edge. There was no memory of doing anything so awful but
maybe—dazed, in pain, and probably in danger—he had
pushed. If he'd seen the man was going to hit him, if he
needed to defend himself, well, it was logical, wasn't it? Even
excusable?

I killed him.

Kill or be killed.

Rob shut his eyes and put his head down on folded
arms. It had always been an intellectual question, whether or
not he could kill in defense of his own life or that of someone he loved. Now he didn't like the answer he kept getting.
I pushed him over the edge.

Wait until his mom heard, she'd...

She'd *what?*

*Didn't Mom once attack a woman in Hot Springs who
was trying to kill Henry? Had she taken time then to worry
about whether or not her vicious attack might end that woman's*

earthly life?

What his mother had been thinking right then was never part of any re-telling he'd heard. Had it been simply a rush of action to save someone she loved, with no time to think at all?

Maybe that was what happened here...an animal urge to save my own life.

He just didn't know.

So tired. Who could sleep well on rocks? Thirsty—hard to swallow. Either have to look for water inside that cave opening or attempt a descent soon.

Can't give in to despair.

Without willing it, his thoughts went back to childhood Sunday school, and to what his mother had taught him.

Does prayer really work? Well, it works for Mom.

He could hear her voice saying: "God takes care of you, wherever you are."

Well, if that's true, why am I up here with a bump on my head?

Because I climbed up of course—my idea, not God's.

How stupid could a man get?

After a few minutes of silence, Rob slid over to the center of the shelter and began poking his fingers through the dust welling up through the gap in the fallen sheet of rock. Who knew, he might dig out an important artifact. The man with the pick obviously thought it possible.

Wait, wait, what was that? He stayed absolutely still and listened. A metallic banging. *Bang–bang–bang.* Silence. *Bang-bang-bang.* Seemed to be coming from inside the cave.

Hallucination? *Bang-bang-bang*, silence. *Bang-bang-bang*, on and on and on.

Rob crawled to the cave opening and called, "*Hello... hello.*" No answer. Of course not.

He went back to pushing his fingers through the dust and bits of rock, working steadily at that while the banging continued, over and over in the same pattern. Something blowing in a breeze, hitting another something? Cave formations often rang like metal when struck. The sound seemed to be echoing through rock corridors until it reached him. It was so regular, a human sort of sound.

His fingers hit something sharp and slick, erasing thoughts about banging. He wiggled the object out of the dust and squinted at it. Looked to be a stone scraping tool. Dalton? Few examples of that culture had been found in this park. He turned the piece over and over in his hands. Eight thousand years ago a woman probably sat here and cleaned animal hides with what he held. But how did *she* get up here? He pictured...Autumn Moon, and his eyes stung with salt. Where was his Autumn Moon?

But wow, he'd proved there were things to find under this rock. Just wait until he could tell Dr. Fletcher, just wait...

Rob dusted the back of a hand across one thigh, then swiped it over his eyes, feeling moisture.

In the several minutes of stillness that followed, he realized he no longer heard the hypnotic banging. Bird calls, rustling leaves—that was all.

He went back to searching along the dusty split in the rock and, after an hour or so had passed, the sharp memory of banging faded. He decided he must have imagined it. Head wounds did funny things.

Keep sifting. Who knows what's here, maybe more evidence of ancient bluff dwellers.

Heard something else. His heart began thumping furiously.

Silence. He *must* be hallucinating.

Then the sound he had imagined came again.

"*Rob McCrite! Rob McCrite!*"

What?

"*Rob McCrite, helloooo, Rob McCrite. Can you answer me?*"

The cell phone rang and Henry's voice said, "Carrie, where are you now?"

"Almost to the turn-off on Highway 65. Why? Do you have news?"

"Rob's been found, he's safe."

"Oh, Henry..." She started crying and after a couple of minutes Shirley's voice came on the phone. "Henry, what is it?"

"Rob's safe. Why is she crying? I didn't mean to make her cry. All I said was that he'd been found. I don't know how else..."

"Don't you worry, those are tears of joy, she'll get collected in a minute. I've pulled off so we can talk safely. Where is he?"

"They've taken him to the hospital in Harrison, just to check and be sure he's okay, you know. They'll probably keep him there overnight. He did get a nasty crack on the head and he's a bit dehydrated, but other than that, they tell me everything looks good. I thought you might want to go directly to him. I've got directions."

"Aren't you with him?" It sounded like an accusation.

"No, I..."

"We'd best hurry then. Wait a minute, I'll find something to write on. Here's Carrie, she's okay now. You can tell the rest of it to her."

The tears had stopped. "Oh, Henry, I am so grateful. Is he all right?"

"Yes, he is. He got trapped in a rock shelter near the top of a bluff. Climbed up, couldn't get down. And what's really odd is that someone evidently hit him on the head while he was in the shelter. They haven't figured out what happened yet because he was still a bit fuzzy when the rescue team brought him out. I gather they dropped ropes from the bluff top to get to him, and that was hair-raising in itself. No one really knows how he made it up the last few yards below the shelter. Sheer rock. I didn't see it, but the description they gave me sounded terrifying. Gutsy man, your son."

In her relief, Carrie could say, "And very foolish, I gather. So, you didn't mention Catherine being in the hospital too. She's okay then? Are you two there with him?"

"No, Carrie, I'm in the park. Rob was alone in that shelter. Catherine is still missing."

"Oh, no, oh, dear heaven, Henry! Couldn't Rob tell you where she might be?"

"He says they got separated. He feels pretty bad about that. Blames himself for all that's happened, and for the fact she's missing. You might be prepared to help him over that hump. Like I said, he was a little woozy when I saw him in the park, but still babbling about Catherine and it being his fault. He knows—everyone knows—he was foolish to climb all the way up to that shelter, but we don't know the rest of the story yet. When we find Catherine and she's safe, he'll get over it quickly enough. But, right now..."

"All right, I understand, and Shirley and I will be praying while you keep looking. Surely Catherine will turn up soon. Any clues as to where she might be yet?"

"No, no sign of her anywhere, though Rob could give us a general idea about where she was when he hiked off and left her."

"*Left her?* Well, now, I *will* give him a good talking to. "

"No, you won't, you won't want to when you see him. He's already piling enough guilt on his shoulders. Carrie, I couldn't be more serious, he needs help thinking this through right now, and a lot of compassion. You'll know what to do and say."

"All right, Henry, and thank you." She glanced at Shirley, who had turned to look out the window. "I love you, Huggy Bear. I'm really sorry I wasn't more of a good sport about the camping, I..."

"Little love, your son is feeling enough remorse for all of us right now, so quit that. It was just fine you stayed home. I missed you terribly, I won't deny it, but I realize now it's okay if we have a few different interests. They wouldn't let me help search for the kids, so I did a lot of thinking while I waited for reports. I finally figured out you need some time alone, without a big, bumbling man always in your way."

"Oh, Henry." She started crying for the second time.

There was a pause before Shirley came on the phone. "Henry, you can give me directions to that hospital now."

"I messed up again. I can't figure out how to say things to her."

"Don't worry about it, this is a tough time for both of you. Y'know, Henry, it takes a while to learn how to be married, whether you're twenty-five or sixty-five, and from what I hear neither of you had much experience at a real marriage before. So just keep on bending a little, and give it time.

"Now, how about those instructions?"

Chapter 11

"THESE PLACES BEWILDER me," Carrie said as she studied the labeled windows in what she assumed was the hospital lobby.

Shirley, right behind her, said, "I always get lost in hospitals—too many halls. Except that one in Eureka Springs was different. It was okay, being small. And weren't the folks there nice, right up to using painted butterfly bandages for repairing the cuts on your cheek?" When Carrie didn't answer, she continued, "Whooee, getting you and Henry married was some adventure. I'll never forget it."

"Me neither," Carrie said, as they walked up to a window labeled *Admissions.*

After Carrie identified herself as Rob McCrite's mother, the woman on duty clicked computer keys and informed them the patient's physician had requested a private room, where he should be by now. She gave the room number and pointed to a hallway. "Dr. Ellington didn't say no visitors, so off you go," she said.

Rooms seemed to be numbered logically, and when they approached the room listed for Rob, they could hear his voice, which made finding the room doubly easy. Peering around the doorway, Carrie saw her son dressed in a green hospital gown, sitting on the edge of the bed with his bare feet dangling far above the floor. He was arguing with a nurse who outweighed him by at least fifty pounds. "I don't *want* to lie down, the back of my head is what hurts. And I don't want to stay here. If you'll just find my clothes, I can get rid of this ridiculous dress and..."

He looked up when Carrie and Shirley stepped through the doorway. "Mom?" He groaned.

The nurse turned and smiled at them. "His mother?" She looked from Carrie to Shirley. When Carrie nodded, she said, "As you can see, he's feeling quite chipper, but Doctor wants him kept overnight for observation since he got a nasty bang at the base of his skull. Maybe *you* can talk some sense into him, so I'll leave you folks alone while I check on my other patients. The nurses' station is just out there—holler if you need me."

Carrie didn't think a hug would be appropriate at the moment, but as soon as the nurse left the room, she walked over to her son and put her hand on his arm. "What happened?"

"How did you know?"

"Henry called."

"Oh." After an awkward silence he said, his voice flat, "Did you...have you heard...any news about Catherine?"

"Not yet. How do you feel?"

"Guess nothing is broken, and after I got some liquid in me, that part was okay. But Catherine..."

Shirley, who had just lowered herself into one of the visitor chairs, stood and said, "Why don't you tell your mother what happened. I'll go for a walk."

For a minute Carrie wanted to throttle her friend, but then realized talking it out was probably exactly what Rob needed.

"Yes, tell us, but first swing your feet up. You can sit in the bed, you don't have to lie down." She propped his pillow upright against the raised top portion of the mattress then, when Rob lifted his feet on the bed, she pulled the sheet up to his waist.

After he was settled, he said to Shirley, "You may as well stay. Mom would tell you everything anyway and she might get something wrong."

Carrie and Shirley looked at each other but neither of them said anything, and as soon as they were seated, Rob began talking.

Catherine's body jerked spontaneously when a small rock skittered down the wall next to the boiler. A flashlight search of the ceiling revealed nothing new, nothing that indicated pending collapse. But how would she know if the whole thing was about to drop? She was a lawyer, not a geologist or mining expert. She shook her fist toward the ceiling, shouted, "I want you to know I'll sue you if you fall," and felt better, if no safer.

"Move the boiler, the whole shebang'll come down," the monster had said.

Well, over the last few hours she *had* moved the boiler, one muscle-straining tug at a time. Now it was at least a foot from its original location, a foot closer to one of the tunnel walls, and there had been no cave-in. The ceiling beam still held, supported at one end by the boiler. A small square of wood wedged between the top of the boiler and a large ceiling rock did fall, along with the rock it supported. She was prepared for that, ducking her head and pulling back as far as she could after a final dislodging tug.

And she'd made use of the board, sometimes tucking it in her jacket hood to protect the top of her head if more rocks bounced down. Body bruises in other places weren't worth worrying about. It was nice to have the board, though. Not only did it make a primitive hard hat, it could also be used as a tool, maybe even a wedge to help free her hand.

There had been showers of dust and small rocks with each tug, but no general collapse. She'd hoped the pipe imprisoning her wrist might break loose as she yanked both arms against the weight of the metal tank, but it hadn't happened. The pipe and boiler were discolored, but they didn't look rusty. It was evidently too dry here for rust to weaken the metal.

Surely the monster hadn't assumed she could drag the tank all the way to the opening of the cave? Why, then, had he bothered to say the ceiling would collapse if she moved it? He must have known that she and the tank wouldn't be traveling any long distances.

What had happened to him? After he'd been gone about fourteen hours—at two A.M. by her watch—she'd decided he probably wasn't coming back.

Sure, her mind acknowledged that he could still return, but it had been so long, and each hour brought increasing conviction that he wouldn't be back. When thoughts about him crept in, her emotions bounced between relief and despair: relief that she had escaped a threatened horror, despair because he was the only living human who knew where she was.

She shook her head vigorously, chasing monster thoughts away, and studied the wall she was moving toward. It appeared to be a solid piece of rock except in one place, where a quirk of nature or maybe a miner's pick had formed an indentation in the wall. The inside of that niche was made up of smaller rocks that looked as if they were set in mud mixed with concrete. Who knew what caused that? An ancient seep of water, dissolving limestone? She'd already discovered the substance was brittle and plaster-like. More important, it chipped when she pounded at it. Rob would know what the stuff was. Oh, Rob...

NO, she wasn't going to let despair take over. She *wasn't*.

That niche in the wall might not mean anything in the long run, but right now it offered the only bit of stability in her tiny and very shaky world. It also offered a goal.

When she'd moved close enough to touch the wall with her right hand, she began using a large rock to pick at the niche, hoping to chip out a larger area—one big enough to hold her body. She hit protruding rocks until one loosened. Then, using her hand and the piece of board, she pried the rock free and dropped it in the scooped-out place in the floor she'd been using for a toilet. Quite a tidy arrangement.

It didn't matter that the process was snail-slow. She had nothing but time.

Of course her brain realized this action could be destabilizing the tunnel, but at least it was action. Sitting quietly with nothing to do but turn the charging handle on her flashlight wasn't an option she could accept. Any action was better than that.

Her first real activity here had been banging on the boiler, sending a signal to anyone who might be listening. When her arm and wrist rebelled after an hour of banging and there had been no answer, she decided to re-think. Cutting the niche was her next idea. It beat sitting in a dungeon and waiting for some kind of end. For discovery? For death?

She thought there was some chance her rock wall would hold if the tunnel ceiling caved in. She'd noticed when the monster carried her here that side tunnel cave-ins they passed hadn't filled all the open area. They left space at the top. If she pulled the boiler loose and the ceiling did fall as predicted but her part of the wall held, she could cover her mouth and nose and shelter in the niche. Then, assuming the cave-in broke the pipe loose and freed her hand, she'd climb out on top of the rubble. *Well, why not?*

But, before she tried the big tug that might free her—or crush her body under tons of rock—she'd have to complete her niche. Then she would have a chance to live.

After all, what did the monster know about collapsing mine tunnels? Maybe no more than she did.

During her first few hours in the tunnel she'd been sure he was going to come back any minute. She'd held her breath at each tiny sound and listened for approaching foot-steps until it seemed her ears hurt. Now she was wondering what had happened to him after he walked off and left her alone in this dungeon.

Dungeons. Sometimes medieval people must have died in them only because they couldn't stand the darkness or the stone walls that seemed to get closer every time they opened their eyes.

At least her dungeon wasn't damp. It was dry as dust and...bones. Dry as bones. For a second she saw her own bones lying on bits of red blanket covered in dust. Who would find them?

NO. Don't think like that, Catherine. You are a fighter, a MacDonald. You are your mother's daughter.

Tears threatened, so she began a guessing game about what might be on the surface of the ground above her. Most likely trees and scrub brush. Wildflowers? Sure, there would be wildflowers. No buildings, though. If a home or other building where people gathered lay above her, wouldn't they have heard her banging? Or, was she just too far underground? She didn't think so. Rob said dry caves were often near the tops of Ozark hills, and this one was certainly dry.

She picked up her hammering rock and hit the boiler, more in anger than in any hope for a response.

Another shower of dust fell from the ceiling. So what. The whole darn ceiling could come down for all she cared, but...not quite yet. She had to be ready.

Catherine looked at her watch. It had now been twenty-seven hours since the monster left. Was his business more demanding than he expected? Surely he hadn't forgotten the woman he held captive. Maybe he found someone younger and more appealing. She snorted and glanced down at her body. Not exactly Ms. Pin-up. Dust covered her jacket and every inch of exposed flesh. A few muddy streaks decorated the jacket front. Tears had caused those, spilling precious moisture on the fabric. When she realized crying was moisture loss, she stopped crying.

There was also one large muddy spot where a drop from her water bottle had fallen. She'd been more careful with her sips after that happened. One tiny sip every few hours. Two sips when she took a bite of cookie or fruit bar.

The sandwich was gone, half of it eaten yesterday for supper, the other half at two this morning. It was just as well she'd finished it. Peanut butter made her thirsty. The fruit bar was better, didn't take so much water. After that was gone, after the water was gone...

When they found her, it would probably make headlines, and she wouldn't even be around to enjoy her hour of fame.

No, no, she would be here, she *would*.

Once more Catherine played the flashlight beam over the mine tunnel walls. Rocks. When she got out of here, she never wanted to see another cave, never another rock wall.

When she got out. "WHEN, WHEN, WHEN," she shouted.

"WHEN, WHEN, WHEN," echoed along the tunnel, fading eventually into the conquering blackness.

She turned off the flashlight, pulled the blanket over her shoulders, and slumped against the tank. It wobbled, and a rock fell, hitting her shoulder. She ignored it, and defiance shrank into numbness as she sat, thinking nothing because she was afraid of her thoughts.

"Rob..."

Did someone say his name? She lifted her head and listened, but heard only the skitter of another rock.

Rob. What was he thinking right now? What was he doing? Was he looking for her? Surely people would be looking for her by this time.

She threw off the blanket and turned on her flashlight. She didn't have time for hopeless day-dreaming and no time for despair. She only had time for work.

She picked up her rock, began hitting at the next piece she wanted to remove from her safety niche, and wondered, for the hundredth time, what Rob McCrite was doing right this minute.

Chapter 12

"YOU CAN SEE it's my fault Catherine is missing." Rob's voice, flat and unemotional, finished the telling of what happened at Rush.

Silence filled the room. No breath whooshed, no little finger moved. Out in the hall, feet clad in rubber-soled shoes squeaked by. Voices murmured.

Finally Shirley shifted in the visitor's chair and Carrie glanced in that direction. Her friend's expression was carefully bland. Carrie hoped her own face looked as placid. *But how could Rob have been so foolish, so...so self-centered? This was the male child she'd given birth to, nursed and nurtured, watched grow to manhood. How could he put himself in such danger? Why did he leave Catherine to fend for herself in unfamiliar country?*

Henry had said Rob felt guilt and concern, but now he seemed almost uncaring. She wanted to shout, pinch him, even slap him, get him to wake up. It was as if he'd frozen inside. A bad sign? What was he really thinking?

The silence continued. Rob looked at his hands, at Shirley, and then at her.

What could she say? Something must be said. What?

Shirley spoke first, her voice calm, normal. "Well now, I think I'll go find me a cup of coffee. Can I bring you something?" After both shook their heads, she slipped out of the room.

Rob stared down at the sheet and repeated in the same flat voice, "It's my fault. If she's hurt or..." He stopped.

"No," Carrie said. Searching desperately for the right words and not finding them, she stumbled on. "Catherine was on her own. You weren't with her." She almost clapped her hand over her mouth when she realized she'd exposed the accusation she felt.

Rob flinched as if she'd slapped him before he spoke again, passion now warming the pent-up thoughts that came spilling out: "That's exactly the point, I *wasn't* with her. I'll never be able to forgive myself if anything bad happens. Mom, I went off and left her. I just hurried off, wanting to see what I could find, wanting to be the great explorer. Stupid, stupid!" He moved his legs, bending them at the knees to make a tent under the sheet, then slid them flat again.

"I didn't take care of her." The stricken look on his face brought Carrie to the edge of the bed so she could touch his hand, and, when he didn't object, take it in hers.

Words. What words would she say?

"You wouldn't intentionally cause harm to any human. Are you thinking it's a blot on your *manhood* because you didn't take care of her?"

He almost laughed. It came out sounding like *hum-humpf*. "She'd have a fit if she heard me say 'yes' to that. Being an independent woman is as important to her as it is to you. I figured that part out pretty quickly, I just haven't figured out the rest.

"Mom, she's...well, the only descriptive word I think of is quirky. She says and does things that confuse me and I don't know how to respond."

"You could use more quirky in your life, son."

"Yeah, no doubt, but I really don't know how to say or do the right things when I'm with Catherine, and I sure don't know how to handle quirky.

"I've been scared for a long time that I'm too much like Dad. You know, detached from everyday life, focused on career; and I guess I did turn out that way. Out there at Rush I was so absorbed in my own interests I didn't think about Catherine's safety. I hiked off and left her alone to face... whatever's happening to her now.

"One of the rangers told us the county sheriff shut down a meth lab in the area only a couple of weeks ago, and...oh God, oh dear God, Mom, I'm frightened. I've gotta get out of this hospital so I can look for her. I can't just sit here." Tears began streaming down his cheeks, and he lowered his head again.

Carrie hadn't seen her son cry since he was a little boy, and it was all she could do now not to cry herself. She continued holding his hand for a few moments, then walked around the bed to retrieve a box of tissues. She handed them to him, one after the other, until the tears stopped and he could talk again.

"Mom, I'm absolutely no good with women. I don't know how to...how to, well, how to *anything*."

Carrie prayed for the right words.

"You were friends with your colleague Jane, and she's obviously a woman. I thought you cared for each other since you dated for over a year."

"Yes. But it was never serious. We were just what you said, friends. Frankly, we eventually got bored because we were both more interested in our careers than each other. All we talked about was our classes, our research. I never thought of anything more back then, never wondered if I'd make a good husband.

"Mom, why would Catherine ever want to marry me now? She has a good life on her own. And look how I treated her."

Carrie was still having a struggle concealing her own emotions, and throwing this at her didn't help one bit. *Marry?* The relationship had moved more quickly, at least in Rob's heart, than she imagined.

God, stay with Catherine, be her shelter, protector, and guide.

Giving herself more time to think, Carrie put her purse down on the foot of the bed and went to bring a visitor chair closer to Rob. He was silent, head bowed. The only thing that moved was his hand, twisting and untwisting a corner of the sheet. Shirley, cup of coffee in hand, walked by, glanced in the room, and disappeared down the hall.

"Rob, did you know much about American Indian history when you were five?"

"Huh? No, of course I didn't." He lifted his head and stared at her.

"How about when you were ten?"

"Well, no, except for my model Indian village. Do you remember it?"

"Of course. Your dad bought that for you when he was in Chicago on business. Toy department, Marshall Field's. Not his normal place to shop."

"*He* bought it for me? Did I know that?"

"He never said anything. I should have told you it was his gift alone.

"After that do you remember when you began taking Indian history seriously, studying into the night, looking for facts and descriptive details?"

"Oh, yes. Middle school, second year. Mrs. Lake's class. I was writing a paper for American History and found a book in the library that went back twelve thousand years or more—the ice age, Paleo-Indians. It fascinated me. What's that got to do with..."

"Then, after high school, you focused on earning your bachelor's, master's, and doctorate. It took a long time."

"Well, yes, but why...?"

"You've studied almost constantly for close to twenty years. Do you see what I'm saying? You haven't taken time to think much about anything else, about how to get along with people outside your field.

"A large part of that is my fault. It didn't bother me that you weren't running around with the other kids. When you didn't go to all the social events your classmates were going to, I was actually glad. Drugs, drinking, smoking, sex— those weren't things I had to worry about like other mothers did. I see now that while you were working so hard to become a college professor, studying anthropology, Indian history, all that, you were missing out on relationship lessons. I should have seen to it you attended at least some parties and dances during your teens."

He shook his head, and his smile held a tinge of sadness. "Most of the time I wasn't asked."

"I'm sure it was only because everyone knew you weren't interested. But now that you've succeeded in reaching your education and teaching goals, it's time to work on relationships."

"Well, yes, but it's easier said than done." He blushed, then laughed. "I don't mean sex, I think I've got that part figured out pretty well. But I want to do and say what Catherine likes. I want us to understand each other and share... things, and I don't know what...I don't know how."

He floundered to a stop, then began again. "I guess women and men are very different, I mean in thinking, not just the obvious physical things. Is it important to know about this Mars and Venus stuff?"

"Maybe. But what's more important is recognizing and then really feeling love and caring. Of *course* women and men are different in a lot of ways, physiological and mental, but they are alike in the need for love and understanding, Catherine no less than you.

"Now here's a tough question. Think before you answer. Exactly why did you hike off and leave her?"

"I've already thought about that, over and over. I was too involved in my interests, in...*myself*."

"Okay, tell me more."

"I was eager to find something at the Buffalo that hasn't been discovered yet. Historical sites there have been robbed by amateur curio seekers and professional looters for many years, making it difficult or impossible for archeologists and historians to match up the few remaining bits and pieces and understand past lives. So much knowledge about human development patterns and our earth environment is still hidden from us because we *are* seeing only bits and pieces, not complete pictures from intact sites."

He shifted into teaching mode so easily, Carrie thought. *That could be off-putting to a woman. Phooey, it's sometimes off-putting to me. I wonder how Catherine feels about being treated like she's one of his students?*

"So, why did I leave Catherine? I was totally focused on the hope I'd be the one to locate a site no one has seen for thousands of years. I didn't think about her, that's the huge and terrible truth."

"Well, a focus on discovery does sound worthy, even if a bit lopsided."

"What makes it worse, Mom, is that Catherine seems truly interested in all this. I feel she understands the importance of our historic past. So, why wasn't I willing to share? Why couldn't I..." His words were cut off by a choking sound. "For all I know, she's suffering horribly right now because of my mistakes, and my chance for real happiness with her is gone."

Oh, dear heaven, Carrie thought. She glanced out the window and saw Shirley standing in the hall.

"There's Shirley. I'd better tell her I'll be a few more minutes. She might want to wait for me in the visitor area." Carrie went to the door, her back to her son while she and Shirley spoke briefly. Shirley nodded and walked away.

Rob had shifted position in the bed and was staring at his mother when she came back in, his eyes displaying some new emotion she couldn't identify. He still wasn't happy with himself, that much she easily understood.

Carrie sat in her chair again, listened once more for ideas, then said, "Your chance for developing friendship or something more with Catherine isn't gone. Recognizing the problem is a major step toward fixing it. The next step is being sorry and saying so, which you have done here and must do to Catherine when you see her. Maybe all this sounds too simple, but once you decide you really want to change, you only have to get busy doing it.

"You're a smart man, but changing direction is going to take more than intellectual thought. It will take real love, including the warm, hugging kind of love. It will take unselfish giving and sharing. If you're thinking about marriage, then that kind of love is already opening up in your life." She stood and took her purse from the foot of the bed.

"Son, why did the doctor put you in a private room?"

"Oh, I guess because I was raving about Catherine and

he thought I was off my head. He said I needed peace and quiet."

"Your mother agrees with him, but not because I believe you're off your head. You should stay here because you do need quiet time for thinking. You'll have to listen and let go—begin a mental free fall into a new way of seeing and doing. I had to do that after your dad died and I moved to Arkansas. You can do it too.

"It's time for us to go find Henry now, but before I leave I want to be quiet for a moment." She shut her eyes.

After a pause, Rob's excited voice broke into her thoughts. "*Mom*, I just remembered something. This morning in the bluffshelter I heard banging. It sounded like it was coming from the cave that opened into the back of the shelter. It went 'bang-bang-bang' pause, 'bang-bang-bang.' Over and over. It was so regular. It must have been a human-made sound. It stopped after a while and I forgot about it until now. Do you suppose it could have been Catherine? Tell them...tell them."

"I will. Do you have your cell phone so we can keep in touch?"

"Whoever hit me stole it. They may have found it on that man lying below the bluff. I forgot to tell you about him."

"You told us about the dead man when we first got here and you were describing what happened."

"There's more. I mean, I must have pushed him over the edge. If he was the one who hit me, maybe I fought back. Maybe I killed him."

"Of course you didn't, you've never reacted in anger like that before."

She couldn't help thinking, *He couldn't kill anyone. He's an academic, for goodness' sake—an intellectual thinker, even a pacifist. He isn't at all like his mother, who sometimes takes action before her thoughts are fully engaged.*

"This is different. It may have been self-defense, but Mom, I don't like feeling I might have killed someone for any reason."

"Did they mention the dead man after they found you? While they were bringing you here?"

"N-nooo."

"And you have no idea how he really died. Well, don't borrow trouble then. You have better things to think about.

"I promise to call you any time there's news, and I'll check in the morning to see when we can come pick you up." She pointed to the phone by his bed. "I have my cell phone if you need to call me."

"Catherine..."

She squeezed his hand. "I'll tell the rangers about the banging you heard. That may very well lead them to her." She smiled and winked in an attempt at cheerfulness she was far from feeling, and then went to join Shirley.

Chapter 13

A S SOON AS HIS MOTHER was gone, Rob rang for a nurse, and when she came, asked for a phone book. She gave him a skeptical look, so he said, "I'll be leaving here tomorrow and I want to learn more about Harrison while I have the time. You know, restaurants and all."

"I'll see," she told him, and left the room.

Rob lifted the lower part of his body, reached down, and pulled out what he'd been sitting on. He laid it on the top sheet and studied it. Thank goodness he'd taken the right credit card, the one from his mom's college that only listed her initials and McCrite.

There wasn't much money, a twenty and some coins. He'd had to grab quickly and didn't have time to check what she had left in her purse. Enough, he hoped.

Rob stared at the card and money. He'd actually stolen from his mother. The wry laugh that burst out startled him, and he looked through the door glass. No one out there to hear him.

So now I'm a thief as well as a killer. Heat surged into his face and the back of his head throbbed. *But I have to get out of here, I have to go back to Rush. How else could I have man-*

aged that? I'll pay Mom back, and she has another credit card with her, I saw it in her purse.

The words sounded reasonable, just like killing in self-defense sounded reasonable.

What else could he have done? When the ranger brought him to the hospital, a nurse took away his billfold and pocket change, "for safekeeping." Thank goodness no one on the emergency room staff found his driver's license. He usually kept it in a slit pocket inside his waistband when he was hiking in back country. A quick look at his clothes not long after they brought him to this room proved the license was still there. That, and what he'd taken from his mom's purse, offered his only way back to Rush.

Mom. Wouldn't she have done the same thing if she were in his place? After thinking for a moment, he decided she would have.

Rob slipped the credit card and money into his night stand drawer just seconds before the nurse came back. She held out a phone book.

As soon as they were in the elevator Shirley asked, "He gonna be okay?"

"He *is* okay physically. I may have given him too much to think about though."

"Because of...?"

"Because of Catherine, and it's much more than the fact he abandoned her. Shirley, he's fallen in love with her, or at least thinks he has. That would be wonderful, except he's still like a teenager when it comes to relationships, and I just realized it's my fault. I encouraged academics instead of social skills when he was growing up."

"Oh, shoot, maybe you did some of that, but he's long since been old enough to think for himself."

"I suppose, but he's in a muddle right now, and I made a few suggestions."

"Kinda dangerous ground, seein' as how he is grown. He'll get around to figuring out the man-woman thing eventually. Unless you think maybe..."

"He's not gay, if that's what you mean. I'd know, simply because we talked about that a long time ago and he's aware I'd still treat him the same, love him just as much. Besides, he cares for Catherine like a heterosexual male would." She sighed. "But I'm not forgetting our foremost concern, and certainly his, is finding her."

"Okay, let's get to it," Shirley said as they walked across the parking lot. "You gonna call Henry now?"

"That's next, then we'll find a grocery store."

As they left the store, Shirley asked, "Shouldn't you phone in about your missing credit card?"

"No, I don't need to. I've been thinking about it, and I'm sure it's not lost or stolen. I haven't opened my billfold since I left home, and my purse hasn't been out of my sight. After the first panic I remembered that yesterday I had the card out when I ordered a jacket from Penney's catalog. I'm sure I left it on my desk. And I have the other card with me, all I need."

Henry was at the Tyler Bend Visitor Center when his cell phone rang. He'd walked up to the center for the fifth time that day, hoping at each trip there would be good news. There wasn't.

Hearing Carrie's voice, he asked about Rob, then answered her still-unasked question by saying there was no news from the searchers.

"Henry, I think I have helpful information about where

Catherine might be. It's from Rob. Is someone there who can tell the people looking for her what he said?"

Henry didn't waste time asking what the information was; he just passed the phone to Shane Lind who listened, making notes. The intensity of Shane's interest gave Henry the first feeling of hope he'd had since learning that Rob—but not Catherine—had been found.

After the ranger handed the phone back and hurried into the office, Carrie told Henry about the banging noise Rob heard. She sent him a kiss just before Shirley's voice came on, asking only for driving instructions to his camp-site.

That was it. Henry clicked the phone off and thought: *It's as if any time we waste talking causes delay in finding Catherine.*

He pushed the visitor center's side door open and walked out on the deck. Trees marked the path of the river far below, with bluffs and hills towering beyond it, but he wasn't in the mood for noticing scenery. He sat on a bench and leaned against the wall, closing his eyes and rubbing two fingers back and forth across his forehead. He felt limp, like he really was Carrie's Huggy Bear and all his stuffing had leaked out. Lack of sleep and worry were catching up with him.

How long had she been missing? Over thirty hours? About that, but of course they had no real idea when she was...what? Abducted? Lost?

He knew too well that the colder a crime gets—if this was a crime—the less chance there'd be of a good resolution.

Oh God, protect her. Help us find her.

His stomach rumbled, and he wondered if Catherine had anything to eat or drink. Rob mentioned a backpack with water and a sandwich, but that wasn't much for this length of time. *Catherine must be hungry and thirsty right now. If she's still...alive.*

Henry opened an eye and glanced down at his hands, realizing he'd begun turning the shiny gold wedding band around and around on his finger.

If only...

If only what? A few months ago I didn't know if Catherine King was alive or dead. Or care.

NO!

Oh, yes, Henry Jensen King, that's true, and you have to face it. You didn't think about her, didn't care where she was.

But then Carrie invited Catherine to our wedding. Now I have a living, breathing sister—and I really do care about her after all.

And now he was left with guilt stretching back through thirty-four lost years, which at times seemed too much pain to endure. "Forgive me," he said aloud.

His stomach rumbled again.

Food. Henry tried to remember when he'd eaten last. *Supper? Yes. Hot dogs. Fixed hot dogs and chili for me and the kids. Threw most of it away when the kids didn't come.*

Breakfast? Can't remember. Wasn't there a breakfast bar and juice? No lunch, though. He looked at his watch. Almost 4:00.

When Carrie got here, what would he say to her? Would she cry? He imagined holding her in his arms and, God help him, crying along with her.

No, no. Now that Rob was safe and Carrie was over crying with relief, she probably wouldn't cry again. But he...

Just what *could* he say to Carrie?

That was the last thought bothering Henry because— eyes closed again, head propped against the building—he fell asleep.

Ranger Lind pointed the way toward the deck and Shirley, who was nearest the door, pushed it open. She stopped so suddenly that Carrie whumped into her back and a gasped *Unh* spurted out.

Shirley put a finger on her lips and whispered, "Asleep. Must be worn out, poor man."

They stood together, looking down at Henry for a few moments, and Carrie couldn't think when she'd loved him more. She wanted to cradle him in her arms.

Well, why not? They'd have to wake him anyway. Slowly, carefully, she sat on the bench, slipped an arm behind his waist, crossed the other in front, and hugged. Then, stretching up, she kissed his chin. Rough. He hadn't shaved today.

"Hello there, Huggy Bear."

He mumbled, "Stuffing leaked out."

She understood. "I'm not surprised. And when did you eat or sleep last? How about we find our cabin and I fix you an omelet, then tuck you in bed?"

He came fully awake and returned her hug and kiss. "Umm, you feel good," he said as Shirley murmured, "Well, look at that!" Surprised, Carrie glanced toward her and saw she stood at the railing looking out over the valley, her back to them.

"I'll be glad to have one of your omelets, my little love. We'll cook at my campsite, though. I need to stay near where news about Catherine will come in. I have the big stew kettle with me, it'll do fine." He got to his feet, pulling Carrie up beside him.

"Omelet?" said Shirley. "Kinda uppity food for a campground, isn't it?"

Ignoring her question, Carrie asked, "Are you hungry?"

"I could eat, yes," Shirley said.

"Okay, I'll make omelets for three. True, I've never made

them at a campsite, but if Henry has a kettle, it'll work."

"Kettle?"

Again Carrie and Henry ignored the question, and the three of them started toward the visitor parking lot.

As soon as Shirley's big old Cadillac was parked behind the blue truck, Henry and Carrie lifted out sacks of food, found the eggs, a package of prepared bacon, and a plastic bag holding onions and peppers. "There's a jar of black olives somewhere in that last sack," Carrie said to Shirley, "and look for the package of shredded cheese and the box of quart freezer bags, please."

"Freezer bags? For leftovers? Here?"

Carrie just shook her head and smiled at her friend.

"Okay, okay, I'll be surprised." Shirley watched in silence while Carrie spread wax paper on the table, put down the kitchen shears and knife Henry handed her, then thumped an onion, a pepper, and the package of bacon on the paper.

"You can help me peel and cut up enough stuff for four omelets if you like," Carrie said. "Henry eats two. I'll do the onion first; I need to cook it a bit." She peeled and sliced an onion, then began cutting it into small pieces with the scissors.

Henry filled his kettle with water, lit the propane stove, and set the water on to boil. He pulled out a small iron skillet and handed it to Carrie. She dumped in a bit of oil and the onion, and then stirred them over heat while Shirley cut up peppers and bacon, using the scissors instead of a knife. "This works pretty good," she said. "Learn something new every day."

Carrie pulled out four freezer bags and held them open while Henry broke two eggs into each bag. Air was squeezed out of the bags, they were sealed, and Carrie and Henry began squishing the eggs to mix them.

Carrie opened a bag and held it toward her astonished-looking friend. "What do you like in an omelet?" she asked.

"Oh, well, I'm not much for peppers, but the rest of what we've got here is good."

"Dump in whatever you'd like."

The three of them added bacon and veggies to the eggs, and each bag was properly re-sealed. After the contents were squished to stir, Carrie took the bags in one hand and held them ceremoniously above the boiling water while Henry looked at his watch. "Go," he said, and all four bags dropped into the water at once.

"Well, I never," Shirley said, and fell silent again.

Henry put a tent-shaped metal frame over the second stove burner and arranged four slices of bread on it. "That's clever," Carrie said. She wondered if bread nearest the fire would burn, but decided not to ask Henry about it.

Henry began alternating between glances at his watch and turning the bread around with a two-tined fork. "Plates and table stuff are in the tent," he told her. "Look to the left. Cans of pop and juice in the cooler. I have instant coffee and tea bags if you want; we can heat water when one of the burners is free. I'll open a can of peaches, too."

Carrie unzipped the door and poked her head in Henry's tent. Daylight glowed through the fabric, covering the interior in soft light. Rather pleasant, really. She found plates, salt and pepper and cutlery, stacked them on top of the cooler, and backed out, pulling the chest behind her.

"Time," Henry said as soon as she returned to the table. "Thirteen minutes exactly."

"Cheese?" Carrie asked Shirley as she spooned bags out of the water.

"I like cheese," Shirley said. Moving quickly, Carrie

opened the first bag and rolled an omelet out on Shirley's plate, following with one for herself and Henry's two. She immediately sprinkled cheese over them. Henry gathered the toast and stacked it on an extra plate.

"I'm gonna fix these for my men," Shirley said. "Easy as falling off a log. They'll sure enough be surprised."

After meal clean-up was finished, Henry got in his blue truck and led the way to a large cabin down the road from the Tyler Bend turn-off.

"Nifty log cabin," Carrie said, walking in from the long covered porch to admire fireplace, kitchen area, bathroom, and loft bedrooms. She set her tote on a chair and pointed at a bed. "Wouldn't you like to take a nap here now?"

Henry put down the two suitcases he was carrying and shook his head. "Couldn't sleep."

"Well, then, come stay with us tonight."

She meant *with me* but didn't put it that way.

"Until Catherine is found, I want to stay around the campground. You know, in case..."

Carrie nodded. He didn't need to complete the sentence.

He looked at his watch. "It's close to dusk, not enough time to drive to Rush. The ghost town is interesting, but as far as the search for Catherine goes, you really can't see anything. The searchers are into rugged country now, way off the roads and regular paths. Shane says they'll search all night.

"Why don't the two of you come back to Tyler Bend with me? We can take folding chairs to the river bank and relax. Today's been tough, tomorrow may be more of the same. A small bit of peace before bedtime sounds good."

Carrie glanced at Shirley, who nodded, then she went to Henry and snuggled against him. "Okay, let's go sit by the river."

Henry went on, speaking as if he were talking to himself. "They keep saying there's nothing I can do to help search. I believe they really mean they don't want me to get in the way, and after being at Rush when they brought Rob out I can see why they think I'd only get lost and add to their problems. It's hard, very hard, but I've stayed away like they asked."

Rob kept his eyes closed and willed himself into silence until the nurse left.

She probably wouldn't be back until time for supper, but he'd better get moving anyway. The rental place closed at six, giving him less than two hours to get out of here and find the agency.

He looked out the door glass. Only one nurse at the station and she was seated, typing on a computer.

He'd already put on his jeans and socks, and now slid out of bed, turned off the reading lamp, and arranged a pillow so—at a glance from the hall—it would look like he was hunkered down under the sheet asleep. Then he hurried to the closet, shrugged out of the hospital gown and into his shirt. *Whew, these clothes could stand washing.*

As soon as his hiking shoes were tied, he glanced out the window again. The nurse was still at her task. He put the credit card and cash in his pocket and shoved his hand after them, hoping the hospital wrist ID wouldn't show above the pocket edge. When he looked out the door and along the corridor, he saw a couple coming toward him and slipped out when they were next to his room. The three of them headed toward the elevators.

As they waited together, he put one hand against the wall to steady himself, hoping the couple wouldn't notice he was a bit woozy.

Finally an elevator binged and the door slid open. Three people in street clothing got out, and Rob and the couple hurried in. So far so good.

The woman pushed a button marked 1 and Rob smiled at her. With any luck that would be the button for the lobby.

He'd planned on taking the stairs. The bing that announced an elevator's arrival might draw attention to an escaping patient, but so far things were going better than he'd hoped.

In less than five minutes, Rob McCrite walked out of the hospital. Smooth as silk.

Using the sun's position and instructions from the man he'd talked to on the phone, he headed toward what must be the right street.

He still felt wobbly. *Move on, one foot after the other. Have to get to the rental place, have to get to Catherine.*

He'd found no car rental agencies listed in the Harrison phone book, but then inspiration hit and he looked for truck rentals. There were several of those. One of them, he soon learned, was located only three blocks from the hospital. So, a truck it would be. Why should he care, as long as it had wheels and a motor that would get him to Rush?

And while he drove he'd ponder the free fall into a new life his mom had urged on him. She was right, he needed a...a... Well, he just needed a more open life.

Rob fingered the credit card in his pocket as he trudged along and thought: *Thanks, Mom. I owe my best effort to you, especially now...and I owe that and more to Catherine.*

Chapter 14

D EAR LORD, GIVE *me a couple of really hard granite rocks.*

Ha! Not likely here.

Catherine began laughing. Well, as long as she was asking for impossibles, a sledge hammer would be much better than rocks.

Or best of all—as long as you're working miracles, Lord—how about a key to fit these handcuffs? And by the way, send along a big bottle of water.

Heck, just transport me out of here.

The laughing stopped. She was being wild and silly, and she knew it but couldn't help it. Even in desperate circumstances she ended up acting silly.

Ah, well, might as well face death with a smile.

Stop that, you ninny. "I, Catherine MacDonald King, J.D., affirm and attest that I refuse to give in. I refuse to die in this mine."

Catherine's shoulders slumped, and she put down the limestone rock she'd been using as a hammer. The handcuffs, though battered-looking, showed no sign of giving up their hold on either her wrist or the boiler pipe. All she had for her labor was a pile of grainy dust and rock chips.

Ah, well. She picked up her flashlight, turned it off, and began winding the handle around and around again. Boy, she could sure write a commercial for this hand-charged flashlight. What would she have done without it?

Gone crazy in the dark, that's what.

Get me out of here, L.L.Bean, and I'll write an endorsement for your flashlight that will sell millions of them.

She turned the light on and studied the niche she'd been chipping. It looked about large enough to shelter her body now, but she'd have to tug the boiler a few inches closer before she could get all the way inside. She still had to stretch to reach the back of the wall. It was going to be a contest. She needed to get the boiler nearer to the niche, but not so close it released the ceiling beam and—as the monster had threatened—brought the whole shebang down. That couldn't happen before she was ready. The cave-in might crush her arm, but a broken arm was better than any alternatives she could think of. If she wasn't badly hurt and the cave-in knocked the boiler pipe loose, freeing her arm, then she could probably climb over the rubble and get out.

Catherine stared up at the ceiling. *I guess it's a good thing there aren't granite boulders here after all. Granite boulders falling from up there would make for one smashed female down here.*

Again she laughed. *Hey, Catherine, be cool. Your crazy streak is getting out of control.*

She studied the chalky, plaster-like material holding her niche rocks in place. *Wonder what that stuff is? The product of some long-ago seep? It's almost like a human made this wall.*

Methodically she began banging away at the back of her niche again. *Just a bit more and...*

Whoa! Without warning, part of the wall disappeared

and her arm shot through into empty space. She fell forward, body following arm, causing the boiler to move a fraction of an inch and rasp against the ceiling it supported.

The stretch of her body jammed her left wrist against the edge of its restraining handcuff. *OW!*

A spasmodic jerk of her right hand released the rock she'd been using for a chipping tool. She heard what sounded like something breaking—a sharp chunk, then clattering.

Stunned, Catherine lay on rocks without noticing their sharp edges. Her free hand and part of her arm were still inside the hole she'd opened, the rest of her body lay against the mine tunnel wall. Her left arm felt as if it was about to come loose from its shoulder.

What on earth has happened here?

She lifted her arm back through the hole, ignoring scraped skin. Then she picked up the flashlight and leaned away from the boiler, holding the flashlight through the hole and wiggling her head back and forth so she could see what the light revealed in the darkness beyond.

It looked like a cave, not another mine shaft. Light revealed a rough ceiling and walls, but no opening into the cave chamber other than the one she'd just made.

Catherine twisted the flashlight toward the floor and saw a row of dusty humps. What...?

They looked like bundles of some kind, each of them two to three feet long and wrapped in coarse burlap. Bundles of what? Her mind resisted the answer that pricked at her.

She stretched closer to the hole, pulling against her already painful arm. Then, among disintegrating bits of burlap, the light found and identified exactly what one of the bundles held. She gasped and thought she shrieked, but the only noticeable sound was a barely audible croak.

A face! Shriveled, pork-rind-looking skin stretched over a miniature skull, dark and dust-covered.

Her eyes scanned the humps again as she tried to remember what Rob said. Didn't he mention the possibility of burial caves? Dear Lord, she must be looking at a burial cave full of children.

Catherine pulled back, leaned against the wall, shut her eyes, and spent a few minutes breathing in huge gasps.

There was no smell of decay. It was far, far too late for that. She only smelled dust, and something she would vaguely define as age—maybe like an old woman's clothing, laid away for years in an attic.

Whirling curiosity drew her to the hole again. This time she willed horror into the background and, beginning at the back wall of the room, started a corpse-by-corpse survey.

Round clay bowls sat beside six of the tiny bodies lying next to the opposite wall. She decided her dropped rock had smashed similar bowls just under the hole she'd opened, but she couldn't get close enough to look through the wall and down.

Another row of five bodies had small spear-like tools beside them. Most of the spear handles were intact, and she could see chipped stone points, a couple of them still bound to their handles with what looked like rawhide. Most of the coarse fabric covering all the bodies was intact too, though holes showed here and there, exposing leathery skin underneath. To her untrained eye the contents of the room seemed remarkably preserved for whatever its age might be.

The wrapped bodies she could see had tiny roundish bumps lined up in swirled loops draped on top of them, and more of the tiny bumps were scattered on the cave floor. Catherine's mind said *beads*. She wondered what they were made of.

There was one adult form in the middle of the room. *Maybe she—or he—is a babysitter, put here to accompany these children into whatever future life their parents imagined they were entering.*

Oh, dear God—their parents. Tears began streaking down Catherine's cheeks as recognition of both the significance and sadness of what she was seeing rolled over her.

When were these children wrapped so very carefully and laid in rows here? Did they all die at once, victims of some terrible disease or tragedy?

Rob hadn't mentioned anything like that happening around this area. But then, how would he or anyone else know about it? There had been no evidence until right here, right now.

Pottery she saw in the room was undecorated and, to her mind, primitive-looking. Rob had shown her pictures of larger pots that were similar. *When did American Indians in this area begin making pottery?*

Late Archaic, hadn't he said? Around 600 B.C.E.

She remembered the date because of her mother's fascination with Bible characters and the history surrounding them. Her mother hadn't been especially religious, and Catherine never saw the inside of a Sunday school, but history was history, and a Bible, enhanced by a couple of worn books about the ancient Middle East, was easily at hand in their home.

Instead of bedtime stories featuring fuzzy animals, Catherine often heard about a world populated by Egyptians, Mesopotamians, Greeks and Hebrews. She knew the lives of Abraham, Joseph, Moses, and David. She knew about the birth of the baby Jesus, his life on earth, and the life of Paul.

And, she knew that, in 600 B.C.E., when pottery-making was just beginning here, Nebuchadnezzar II had a fancy palace in Babylon. That's why she'd remembered the pottery date, because she wondered about the contrast in development between American Indian pottery and what she pictured as gold wine bowls belonging to Nebuchadnezzar and his court.

"Two different worlds," was all Rob said in response to her question.

So, I've broken into a burial cave full of children who have been here for at least 2500 years...and Dr. Robert Amos McCrite isn't here to share this terrible, magnificent moment with me. Oh, my, is he going to be put out. I've uncovered a real archeological treasure all by myself.

"Oh, Rob. Where are you? Are you okay, or did the monster get you, too?" She said it aloud, and the sound of her voice startled her, though it was barely audible.

Was Rob looking for her? Why hadn't he heard her banging, then? She'd kept at it for over an hour. To her, it sounded loud enough for anyone on the surface to hear. But, who knew?

How long ago was that? She looked at her watch. *About eight hours? Or was it ten hours?* In spite of the watch, she was beginning to lose track of time. Was it day or night outside? She couldn't remember.

Should she try banging on the boiler again? The best time for that would be during the day, when people might be out and about. *Out there—in the sunlight.*

Catherine leaned her head against the boiler and, without thinking of moisture loss, cried in earnest. When a few salty tears ran down far enough to sting her cracked lips, she realized what she was doing and stopped crying. Then she picked up a rock and began chipping away at the rest of her niche wall.

Chapter 15

CARRIE OPENED HER eyes and looked from Henry to Shirley. Oh, my, the comfortable camp chair, evening sun on her back, and shush and ripple of the river had put her right to sleep. Henry was right. This was relaxing, and both he and Shirley were still busy proving it. Shirley had her mouth open and was almost snoring.

Carrie sent Henry a silent thank you for suggesting this time on the riverbank. For her, at least, it opened awareness that all the horror of today couldn't kill what was beautiful and good in the world.

A constant drumbeat of apprehension had been running behind her every thought and action since she and Shirley left the hospital. *Catherine—Catherine—Catherine.* This strong focus on the evil had blurred her ability to cope with it mentally, let alone think of helpful action for any of them to take beyond what was already being done. Maybe there really wasn't anything physical the three of them—or Rob—could do, but fear and anxiety still had to be dealt with.

She wondered how Rob was doing with his thought re-adjusting. She regretted not reminding him that life-changing adjustments don't happen overnight. Gentle awakening was realistic; a 180-degree turnaround in thirty minutes wasn't.

She considered getting her cell phone and calling him with a few new thoughts. Then, as she watched the river moving smoothly forward, she rejected the idea. Shirley was right, Rob was an adult, capable of growing new ideas on his own. Besides, he'd always been deliberate about everything he thought and did. He'd be the same way while he figured out how to grow his experience with Catherine.

A crunch of footsteps through loose stones announced the arrival of a woman carrying a tackle box and fishing pole. She glanced at the three of them, smiled and winked at Carrie, then took exaggerated tiptoe steps farther away along the riverbank.

While Carrie watched, the woman squatted beside her tackle box, put something green and sparkly on the end of her fishing line, then stood. After a bit of fiddling she flipped the rod back and shot the green sparkly thing flying out over the water, where it came down like a falling leaf. She began turning a crank on her rod that brought the bit of something on the end of the line toward her slowly, then more quickly, and back to slow. Her graceful motions stunned Carrie. The woman was *fishing*. *Was this what Henry did, how he looked?*

Instead of fishing, she might be watching a complex dance. The rhythm of the woman's moves—the slow-quick-quick-slow action on the line, the arching rod and skipping green bit in the rapidly moving water—were all beautifully choreographed.

When the line was wound in, the dance began again, and yet again, much to Carrie's pleasure. She wished she could walk closer, ask about the procedure, maybe even get a look at what was on the end of the line, but the woman seemed wrapped in her own bubble of peace and pleasure. Instinctively Carrie understood that and stayed where she was.

Then the rod jumped and bent sharply toward the water. A fish! Carrie looked away. She didn't want to see what was going to happen next. But in a moment she looked back. The natural end result of this dance had to be faced.

The woman was winding her line in, stopping occasionally to lift the rod and pull against the fish.

And there it came, silvery, about a foot long, flipping up in arched curves to one side, then the other. Dismayed, Carrie anticipated the killing of the fish, and the spoiled memory of grace on a riverbank.

The woman swung the fish into her hand, deftly released it from the hook, and laid the still arching form back in the water. A flash of motion and it was gone. As the woman prepared to cast again, Carrie realized she'd brought no container for fish. There was only the rod and the tackle box.

"She's very good."

Henry's whisper brought Carrie back to earth.

She let out a sigh, turned toward him and said, "That's what fishing is like?"

"A lot of it, yes."

"Oh, my."

They sat in silence for a few moments while Shirley slept on. Then Carrie looked over at him and asked, "Rob told me he saw a dead man on the ground below the bluffshelter. Do you know anything about that?"

Henry's startled look said it all. "No, no one mentioned anything to me. How did the man die? Does Rob know?"

"That's just it, he doesn't know, but he's afraid he killed him."

"Carrie!"

"Well, he says he doesn't remember anything at all after that blow to his head, but believes he could have reacted by shoving the man over the edge. He doesn't like thinking he killed someone, even to protect himself."

"Huh. Well, I'll ask Shane about it in the morning. I'll let you know what he says. Speaking of morning, are we going to get together for breakfast?"

"Sure."

"My place or yours?"

She laughed. "Let's eat at the cabin, but not too early, so you'll have time to ask about the dead man before you come over. You can call me on your cell phone when you're finished here."

A canoe holding a couple and two small children appeared from upriver. Each parent held a paddle, and without visible consultation, they began maneuvering deftly toward the shore, staying as far away from the fishing woman as they could. When they were several yards down river and about six feet out, the man slid into the water and waded toward the rocky shingle, pulling and guiding the canoe while the two children, a boy and girl, shrieked and giggled. Then the children splashed out too and began bobbing around in the shallows. They looked like plump roly-poly dolls in their life vests.

Shirley opened her eyes. "Whooee," she said, "those young-uns are sure having a good time. Makes me wish I'd brought a bathing suit, or at least shorts, so I could go wading, though I'm sure that water's a mite cold.

"Roger 'n me are going to have to come back to this place soon; though when I mention it he'll say, 'What for? We got Walden Creek the other side of our back pasture.'

"Then I'll tell him he should come see where so much history happened. I know Rob can fill me in on enough of that to get Roger interested. He'll come here for the history."

"Oh, my, yes," Carrie said, "Rob can always tell you more history than you want to hear." She stretched her legs out and watched evening shadows work their way along the opposite shore. A bluff that appeared light grey earlier was now shaded from dark grey at the bottom to sun-splashed gold at the top.

"It's so beautiful here," she said. "I want to sit by this river in peace every evening I'm here, and I pray Rob and Catherine will be sitting with us by tomorrow evening."

"Amen," Henry said, and yawned. "I think I'll turn in early. May I escort you ladies back to your cabin?"

Carrie smiled at him. "No, thank you, sir, we *ladies* will manage on our own. We'll even carry our chairs back to your truck."

She stood and, before folding her chair, bent and put an arm around Henry's shoulders. "Sleep well, my love. Tomorrow will surely bring us good news about Catherine."

He stood to give her a proper hug and kiss in spite of the small audience along the riverbank. "I hope you're right, Cara, I surely hope you're right."

Rob blinked his eyes rapidly, tightened his hands on the truck's steering wheel, and tried to picture roads on the map he'd bought at the rental place. Whew, he was getting so sleepy. Hungry, too. Maybe he should stop for something to eat and take another look at that map before beginning his drive to Rush. When a Wendy's sign appeared on the left, he turned off the highway.

A few minutes later Rob drove into traffic again, balancing one coffee cup between his legs while a second cup perched in the center drink holder and a sack with hamburger and fries rested on the seat beside him. Huh, why had he supposed he could drive and eat? It wouldn't work. He glanced toward the shopping mall coming up on his right. If he pulled into their lot, he'd be able to eat safely and also study the map before heading south.

After parking he yawned and wished he had time to stop off for a quick nap in his tent at Tyler Bend. But that would mean a delay in locating Catherine. He knew where she had to be, somewhere in the cave system that opened off that bluffshelter near Rush. He'd find her there, he knew he would, and two cups of black coffee ought to help keep him awake. After eating, he'd head straight for Rush. He could probably make it there in an hour or so.

A few minutes later he stuffed food wrappings and one empty cup in the Wendy's sack and picked up the map. A quick look to get his bearings, and he'd be on his way. The second cup of coffee could come later; he didn't care if it got cold.

Rob chuckled. He was a bachelor. Hot food and drink grown cold didn't bother him a bit. He shut his eyes and tried to picture what *not* being a bachelor might be like. Would he or Catherine do most of the cooking? Come to think of it, he didn't even know if she liked to cook. Well, who cared...he didn't...care...

When he opened his eyes, it was dark. Lights along the highway flashed at him. He must have fallen asleep. Well, no need to worry about that nap now. He'd had it.

He brushed a hand over his forehead, took a sip of cool coffee, and headed for the highway.

A number of miles after the lights of Harrison faded, a hideous thought hit him like a thunder bolt. *Dark!* It was dark, and he had no flashlight. Such a small thing, but without it, any search at night or in a cave would be impossible. For a moment he considered turning back to buy one

in Harrison but discarded that idea as a true waste of time.
That meant the only flashlight he had access to was in his
tent.

So he had to go to Tyler Bend. Surely Henry was sleeping at the cabin tonight. Rob didn't want Henry around to
try and talk him out of his mission. He wouldn't listen, of
course, but right now he couldn't handle even the smallest
amount of friction.

He looked at his wrist, remembered he had no watch,
and wondered what time it was. Probably around eight, or
maybe nine. Rob considered. In another forty-five minutes
he would be at Tyler Bend. The drive from there to Rush
took an hour and fifteen minutes. He'd still be at Rush
before midnight.

For a moment he wanted to swear in frustration because roads around the Buffalo National River weren't direct
routes from point to point. But of course cutting a bunch
of roads would spoil the wildness that everyone, including
himself, wanted to preserve. With all the meandering curls
and bends in the river, a canoe traveled over thirty-five miles
from Tyler Bend to Rush, and it sure wasn't any closer by
road.

Well, no hope for it, he had to get a flashlight. He
turned the truck toward Tyler Bend and made a silent promise to Catherine:

I'm coming.

The first thing he saw when he drove into the campground
was Henry's blue truck parked by his tent. Oh, rats! What
was wrong with that man? He was supposed to be in bed
with his wife. Still, he was probably sound asleep by now, no
need to worry.

Rob pulled into the parking area by the campground

restrooms, slid out of the truck, and clicked the door shut
as quietly as he could. The almost full moon and lights
and lanterns here and there helped him see his way along
the road to his tent. He unzipped the flap, then decided to
check Catherine's tent first to be sure her things were okay.
Besides, she had one of those wind-up flashlights, which
might come in handy if she'd left it in the tent.

A quick check showed him that Catherine's possessions
were as she'd left them, but there was no flashlight. He hesitated when he saw the neatly folded stack of clothing. Might
be a good idea to take fresh things to her. He knew how
tired he was of what he'd been wearing. She'd probably feel
the same way and, even without a shower, would appreciate
clean clothes.

Rob picked up jeans and a shirt and hugged them
against his face. Something of hers... Well, whether she
wanted clean clothes or not, they were a thread of reality
joining him to her living self, wherever she was—a reminder
of what he'd been holding to in thought all along: *She is
alive, and I will find her.*

He started to back out of the tent and stopped. He'd
forgotten about underwear. After a short hesitation he
crawled back in, unzipped her duffle bag, and felt inside. It
only took a minute to identify a bra and pull it out. Feeling
around again he finally touched soft fabric. Must be panties.
Gosh, those things sure slid around, how did she keep them
folded? The contents of her bag were messed up now, and,
in the dark, it would take forever to get it all re-organized.
But, if he didn't, she'd know he'd poked around through her
underwear.

*Oh, don't be stupid, Rob. If you hand her clean underwear,
she'll know exactly where you got it.*

He was backing out of Catherine's tent again when a

familiar voice behind him whispered, "Hey, buddy, what's up?"

Chapter 16

ROB'S YELP OF SURPRISE turned on lights in the trailer occupying the next campsite. In what seemed like seconds, its occupant opened the door and, once more, stepped out to confront Henry. This time he wore white boxer shorts and flip-flops. The beard was noticeably heavier.

"Oh, you again," he said to Henry. "Who did you say you were?"

"He's with me, Al," Rob said, pulling out of Catherine's tent and standing. "This is my, uh, stepdad, Henry. Sorry if I woke you up."

"So you're back, are you? I heard you and the little gal went missing. She okay?"

"We don't know anything yet," Henry said, instinctively cautious. "All we can do is wait. Rob is fine though, and we're getting ready to catch up on our sleep. Thanks for watching over his things while he was gone."

Rob opened his mouth. "Catherine is..." but Henry took hold of his arm and squeezed, hoping that would shut off whatever he'd been about to say.

"Urrr, sorry again, Al. Goodnight. We'll be very quiet."
Smart boy.

"Well, s'okay. You be careful now, y'hear?" Al backed into his trailer, latched the screen door, and disappeared. The light went out.

Henry whispered, "Get your things, including your sleeping bag and pillow. Since there's a bra strap trailing out of that bundle I assume you have some of Catherine's clothes. Hand me her stuff, get what you need, and we'll go to my place. We can talk freely there; my nearest neighbor left today and no one else has taken the spot yet."

Rob didn't seem to notice that Henry hadn't asked why he was holding Catherine's clothing. Without a word he crawled inside his tent.

Henry waited, not really positive Rob wouldn't go off by himself if left alone. Then, arms stacked with gear, they both headed along the road to Henry's tent.

As soon as they were inside, Henry turned on his battery lamp and pointed toward the floor. "We can sit on our bed rolls." As soon as he'd folded down on top of his, he looked around the tent, sniffing. Finally he looked at Rob more closely. "Whew, didn't they bathe you at the hospital?"

"That's not me, it's my clothes. I brought clean to change into. I guess we can put the dirty stuff in your truck—get it out of the tent?"

Rob began pulling off his shirt. "Now, will you please tell me why you're awake and tailing me?"

"Hospital called about thirty minutes ago, woke me up. I gave my cell phone number as contact to the ranger before he drove away with you, but I guess he forget to leave it with the folks in the emergency room or somebody lost it. They discovered you'd gone missing when a nurse's aide delivered your supper, but it took them all this time to find me. They finally called the park's emergency number, and from there got one of the rangers who works in the visitor center at his home. He had my number with him in case any news about Catherine came in."

"Is there...news?"

"No. Hey, don't put those jeans on. Wouldn't you rather sleep in your underwear? I think you should stay here with me. News'll come here first."

Henry held back a laugh when Rob's chin came up. His eyes locked into a *dare me* look as he pulled one jeans leg over his foot. So, he was like his mom in some ways after all.

"I had a nap in the truck. Say, what time is it anyway?"

Henry looked at his watch. "One forty in the morning."

Rob's obvious dismay took Henry by surprise. "Oh, no, I really have to hurry, I slept in that truck lots longer than I thought. I've gotta get to Rush as soon as I can. I know where Catherine is." He lurched to his feet and finished tugging on his jeans.

Henry chewed a cuticle, giving himself time to think. "Rob, hold on. Rangers, volunteers, sheriff's deputies are all over that area looking for her. They're searching through the night, and your mom told them about the banging."

"Can't help it. I have to go myself."

"You're supposed to be in the hospital right now, recovering from a pretty harrowing experience. Are you sure...?"

"I'm fine and I'm sure. So, you going to try and stop me?" Another lift of the chin.

"Nope. I'm going with you." Henry saw Rob's startled look, had expected it in fact, but he ignored the look and went on. "When the hospital called, I was pretty sure this was exactly what you planned. I hoped you'd come here first, but since it took so long for them to find my number, about six hours had passed by the time they called. I didn't see you here, but had no way of knowing if you'd come and gone. I also thought you might have headed straight to Rush. I was about to head that way myself when the rental truck drove in and you got out.

"Why the truck and not a car, by the way? And how did you manage your escape from the hospital? They took your billfold when they checked you in, didn't they? What did you do for money and a driver's license?"

Rob gave him a sketchy account, promising to fill in details once they were on the road.

"We need to call the hospital," Henry said, "and tell them you're okay."

"I'm not going back."

"You won't have to, except to get possessions you left there and settle your bill. Do they have your insurance information?"

Rob nodded.

"Okay, one of us can call them while we drive. They left a number for that.

"Then, we need to tell your mom where we are. She's had enough scary unknowns to deal with this week."

"Can't we leave her a note somewhere?"

"I thought we could call her from Rush at daybreak."

"I don't think there's reception in most of that area."

"Well, I'll write a note then. Let's drive the rented truck, the rangers all know mine by now. We'll park on the road near the cabin she and Shirley are in. One of us can walk in and tie the note to their door. Driving to the yard would probably wake Carrie up—Shirley too. You know what would happen then."

Rob nodded. "They'd try to stop us."

"Not on your life. They'd insist on coming along."

"They would? You sure?"

"You bet. Think about it—you probably know your mom better than I do."

"Maybe we should take them then."

"Definitely not. We don't want them in danger. This expedition could very well be dangerous, have you thought about that?"

Rob nodded.

"We have no idea why Catherine is missing, or—unless she's fallen somewhere—who might have taken her. But," he looked sideways at Rob, "we're both willing to do dangerous things for the ones we love, aren't we?"

Rob stared at him for a minute, then blinked. Leaving the question unanswered, he said, "We need to carry stuff—water, food, flashlights, Catherine's clothes, first-aid kit. My backpack is gone."

"I've got one, and a small duffle. We'll manage to get it all in. I suppose you're thinking Catherine will be glad to have fresh clothing?"

"You bet. I sure was."

"Say, you aren't planning a climb to that impossibly high bluffshelter again are you?"

"No way. Catherine couldn't have entered the cave system from there anyhow. There has to be a ground-level opening somewhere along the base of the bluff."

They stopped talking when they heard a truck start. Henry turned off the lantern and opened the tent flap. "Not your rental, it's okay."

Then, lights off, a dark truck grumbled slowly along the road. As it passed their camp site, Rob said, "That looks like Al's truck."

"Odd man," Henry said. "Wonder where he's going."

"Dunno. Like you say, he's odd. He left during the night the first night we were here, too. That's one reason I wasn't more apologetic about waking him. I bet he wasn't asleep. I think he sleeps during the day."

As the two men began loading the backpack and duffle, Rob asked, "Aren't you going to take your gun with you?"

"Didn't bring it."

"Well, I have a pocket knife with a long blade. Not much of a weapon or even a tool, but it's better than nothing. If Catherine is caught somewhere, we may need more tools, but I don't have anything else with me that we could take.

"Hey, I know where Catherine hides a key under her Jeep. Do you suppose that's still parked at Rush? She has tire-changing tools and a small folding shovel for snow if we can get inside."

Henry said, "Far as I know they left the Jeep where they found it."

"Good. Do you have a pocket knife?"

Henry nodded. "Fairly large Leatherman."

Rob put a hand in his pocket and held out a slender oval tube. "Catherine sometimes carries Mace or pepper spray. She left this in her tent yesterday instead of carrying it.

"No, I'm wrong." He stopped, looking stricken. "It's two days now, isn't it? Well, anyway, she said...she laughed and said she'd be safe with me at Rush, that I...could protect her." After a pause he mumbled, "I found it in her things just now and brought it with me."

Henry nodded. "Okay, can't hurt to have it. I'll write the note while you finish packing."

Ten minutes later the two men left the tent. As they started around the road toward the rental truck, Henry reached out, touched Rob's shoulder and fiddled with the backpack strap resting there, pretending to straighten it. Then he lifted the duffle to his own shoulder and, side-by-side, they strode on.

Chapter 17

"WHY DON'T I DRIVE, Rob? You rest. Sleep if you can. I'll be the one to walk in and fasten our note on your mom's cabin door since I know the lay of the land there. No need for you to do anything until we get to Rush."

Henry was half-surprised when Rob agreed easily, almost too easily. He'd been so on fire with mission that Henry thought an urge to pilot the vehicle taking two gallant knights to save a lady might be part of his mental package.

Seemed not. Maybe he was too tired for protests. After all, he'd had almost no sleep at the hospital. Henry figured the smooth rumble of the truck on the road might help put him to sleep.

It did. When they were only a few miles from Tyler Bend, Rob's head slumped sideways. Truck noise overcame anything that would have been revealed by his breathing, but he was very quiet otherwise. Good. The kid needed rest, and Henry needed time to think.

Don't like the feel of this expedition at all. Too many unknowns. But I couldn't let him go on his own, and no way I could have stopped him. He's wound pretty tight right now.

Guess I should have left a note for Shane as well as Carrie.

Safer, give us some back-up. Maybe she'll tell him, or we'll run into rangers or other searchers at Rush. I'll be glad if we do. I know too well how dangerous it might be for us to go in alone when we have no idea what we're facing.

I'm sorry there was no chance to talk this over with Cara, but I bet she'd have insisted on coming along. I couldn't let that happen.

Catherine. Rob seems sure he knows how to find her. I hope he's right, and we aren't walking into something we can't handle. For her sake and his, we've got to try.

Wish I had my gun.

I suppose he really is in love with her. Kinda awkward about it though. Should I offer advice? Huh, some advisor. But still, Carrie and I, we do okay. He sees that. Wonder what he really thinks about us? His mom and a big, bumbling ex-cop from Kansas City with one failed marriage and one illegitimate daughter on record.

People don't use that term these days. True, I wasn't married to Susan's mother, but, thanks to Carrie, the past has kind of faded away. She said it was time to move beyond what happened over thirty years ago. She was right.

He thought back to when, with Carrie standing beside him, he had watched Susan and baby Johnny—his grandson—get off an airplane. Tears stung his eyes. That was the first time he'd ever seen his daughter, and Carrie's detective work was what brought them together.

Carrie says Rob tried to talk her into marrying me right after he and I met—a long time before the two of us were ready. So I guess he thinks I'm okay.

Sometimes I forget he's already in his thirties, just like Susan. Grown man for sure—Dr. Robert Amos McCrite. But maybe not so smart about loving a woman? Huh. Well, could be he'd like to talk about it. I can start by saying something about my experiences. We'll see what happens.

Best now to think about what's facing us this morning.

How much does Rob really know about cave systems? Suppose we find a meth lab, or...what? He said looters were taking valuable archeological treasures from caves around here. Did Catherine walk in on something like that? But surely she wouldn't try to explore a cave on her own.

I hope I don't end up needing my gun.

Henry stopped the truck as soon as they entered the outskirts of Rush. He had just reached over to touch Rob on the shoulder when the young man stirred and lifted his head.

"We here?"

"Yeah. Time to plan our strategy."

"Umm, okay." Rob yawned. "Well, drive ahead to where the road seems to stop and turn left. Catherine's Jeep should be in the parking lot."

It was, but two cars were there too, a park vehicle and an unmarked white car. Both were empty, and the area seemed quiet.

Henry pulled up beside the Jeep and Rob hopped out immediately. Before Henry could join him, he had dropped to his knees in front of the grill. He reached under, found the key in its magnetic case, and soon had the rear door open.

"Hold the flashlight here for a minute," he said when Henry walked up. With surprising quickness and ease Rob removed the spare tire and retrieved the lug wrench. He handed that to Henry, felt along the side wall of the cargo area, and pulled out a folding shovel. Then he re-locked the door and said, "Guess this is the best we can do for either a tool or weapon on short notice.

"Now we go left along that lane. I'll tell you when to turn in. You'll see a small cleared area by some old concrete piers. We can leave the truck there."

When they pulled in Rob said, "There was a Thunderbird here when we came in yesterday—no, day before yesterday, isn't it? I keep forgetting. Catherine stopped to admire that car before we hiked up the hill."

Henry frowned. "Thunderbird convertible? Maybe '57? Silver?"

"Silver, yes. I'm not good on model years. Looked small."

"There was a car like it down by your tents in the campground. Drove away about dawn early yesterday morning. There might be a connection between that and its presence here where you last saw Catherine. You ever seen that car before?"

"No." Rob put his hand on the door latch. "It couldn't have anything to do with us, could it? There was no one around the car here and we didn't meet anyone. Folks had probably gone off canoeing. Silly thing to drive in rugged country, but then some people are silly. So, are we ready to leave now?"

Not wanting to worry Rob about the car, Henry dropped the subject and said, "Let's plan our strategy first. What's your idea about how we find the cave?"

"There must be a ground-level opening, or something near ground level beyond the bluffshelter I climbed to. I didn't see anything before I got there, so it's farther on. I guess we just keep walking and searching. I...well, we *must* find that opening. It has to be there. Otherwise, how could Catherine have gotten in the cave?"

Henry had to say it. "Assuming she is in there."

"There was the banging..."

"Yes. Okay, lead the way." Rob shrugged into the back-pack, Henry hefted the duffle to his shoulder and, led by flashlight beams, they headed out.

After thirty minutes or so Henry said, "Since we haven't come on any searchers, I guess they've finished looking in this area. I wouldn't mind meeting up with them, but still, we'd best be as quiet as possible. Someone more menacing could surprise us. We'd rather see any strangers first."

"Yes." Rob's reply was only the single word, but Henry heard fear there.

He's suffering a lot over this. Of course he's worried about Catherine, and there's his own fear to deal with, not to mention blaming himself for her disappearance.

I pray she's okay. God help us...help us find her.

Henry shut down thoughts of possible disaster that were beginning to rush in, and repeated to himself, *Help us find her.*

He was puffing when they reached a clearing with a flat-topped rock at one side.

"We can sit here and rest for a moment," Rob said.

Henry sent his flashlight beam around the base of the rock, just to be sure. Pretty white flowers there. No moving critters, especially no snakes or skunks. But...something red caught in the flowers.

He picked up the red circle and pulled at it. "Wonder what this is? Some kind of stretchy thing."

Rob was bent over, elbows resting on his knees, head in his hands. Now he looked up, white face glowing in Henry's light. He held out a hand, touched the red circle, but didn't take it from Henry. "It's Catherine's," he said, voice quivering. "She calls them scrunchies—ponytail scrunchies. She put this red one around her hair before we left our camp." He stood quickly. "She was here. Let's go."

After pushing through undergrowth and slipping on rocks for another thirty minutes, they came to a disturbed patch of ground. Rob looked up. "We're below the bluffshelter."

Henry inspected the disturbed area, but didn't comment when he saw evidence of blood among the rocks. He quickly turned his flashlight away.

"From here on we're in new territory," Rob said. "We're outside the park boundary, at least for the most part. The line wiggles around a bit in this area."

They continued slowly, moving even more quietly than before as they searched the bluff face for openings. Neither of them spoke until Henry laid a hand on Rob's shoulder.

"Clearing."

"I see it." They turned off their flashlights and slid toward the cleared area. Once they were out in the open Rob whispered, "House over there. No lights."

"Occupants asleep?"

They moved ahead, depending only on moonlight now, with Rob leading the way. Still, they were almost on the truck before they saw it.

"Blast, it's Al's," Henry whispered.

"What's *he* doing here?"

"I guess that's one thing we need to find out. Look over there...to the left. See it? Seems to be a garage or some kind of storage building against the bottom of the bluff. Shall we take a look?"

"Yes. You lead. I'm starting to shake."

Henry wished he could see Rob better. "You gonna be okay?"

"I'm fine. It's just that...well, we may be close to Catherine. But Al...why's he here? Do you think he has something to do with her disappearance?"

"Possibly." Henry was taking careful steps toward the

building. When they reached it, he moved along the side and looked around a corner. "Here's a garage door. I don't think we dare try opening it."

"Let's look for another door."

They found it on the opposite side, but it was locked. Rob continued on toward the back of the building.

"There's open space between the garage and the bluff. I'll see what's here." Rob's voice now sounded firm, excited.

Henry stayed where he was, cutting off his natural tendency to insist on checking any unknown area first, or at least going with Rob. Time to leave the man alone.

After several minutes of listening to scrapes, the brush of clothing against metal siding, a couple of clicks, and then frightening silence, he heard a small creak. Turning back he saw a dark shadow at the open side door.

Rob's voice said, "There's a door in the back. It wasn't locked, and this one just has a thumb bolt. Come in and see what I've found."

"Silver Thunderbird," Henry said as soon as he was through the door.

Rob turned on his flashlight.

"Careful with that in case anyone is looking this way. Might be cracks around the garage door, and you already said Al was a night owl."

"Never mind," Rob said, "look here." He pointed the flashlight into the open trunk of the car.

"I didn't see anything inside the car itself and it's locked, but the trunk was already wide open. There's an archeologist's treasure trove in here. See? That's part of a cradle board, and there's matting, some pottery shards and a couple of whole pots. Lots of points. I almost can't believe it. What a find!"

Rob frowned and went on. "Al's gotta be involved in

looting, maybe partnering with one or two others, including whoever owns this property. Groups of looters tend to be small so the profits—and information about where items are located—won't be spread out. In fact it's often only one person, and they're very protective of their territory. Not much sharing going on. It looks like these guys have got a bird's nest on the ground, with property backed up to a concealed cave that must be the source of this stuff."

Rob shut off his flashlight. "I suppose the garage was built to hide the cave opening. We're almost to her, Henry, I know we are. Maybe she surprised Al looting, or one of the others, and they've taken her prisoner. We've got to find her as soon as possible, before they..." There was a long pause while Henry—and Rob, he supposed—filled in pictures of imagined horror.

"Al's probably in there bringing out more items, destroying the tremendous research potential Dr. Fletcher and others would gain were the location left intact as discovered." He halted, looked down, and kicked viciously at one of the Thunderbird's tires before he went on. "You know, we may have to deal with Al before we get to Catherine."

Henry shifted the duffle and tightened his hand around the tire iron. "I hope like heck we don't see him—or his partner. Both of them could be in there. Two vehicles, two men? I should have told someone at the park we were coming here, especially since we're out of cell tower range. Too late now."

Rob started toward the garage's back door. "More likely they're in the house, waiting to move things in the morning. Come on, let's hurry."

Henry said, with more conviction than he felt, "I'm ready. Lead the way."

Chapter 18

FIRST ROB, THEN HENRY, stooped to get through the rock archway in the bluff face, but as soon as they were beyond that, space expanded into a cave room about eighteen feet across. A tunnel opened at one side.

When Henry stood to look around the cluttered area, Rob was already on his knees, frantically picking at bits of cloth mixed with the floor dust. "The freakin' pervert... Look at this! I hope I *did* kill that guy, and I'll be glad to kill Al and any of his other friends." By the time he finished speaking, his words were a raspy squeak.

"Hey, Rob, careful about noise. What have you got there? What is it?"

"Catherine's clothes! Look at this, it's all of them, what she was wearing day before yesterday, even her bra and panties. Shredded, every bit of it shredded. Look, just look!" His hands jabbed through the dust, clutching at pieces of fabric that Henry now recognized as denim and bright cotton. He identified a length of elastic with bra hooks in it, and strips of red lace that must have come from panties.

Rob seized a nearby hand trowel and threw it against the cave wall, then began picking up everything he could find on the floor and throwing it wildly, keening and choking out sobs all the while. Finally he hurled what was left of a broken chair against the rock and it smashed into splinters with an echoing crash. Running out of things to throw, he bent toward the floor as if he were going to be sick, and made huge, gagging noises mixed with inarticulate words.

Henry hurried over and grabbed Rob under the arms, hauled him to his feet, and rolled him against his chest to hold as if he were a woman. Rob's body jerked and flailed, but Henry only tightened his arms. Finally the awful din quieted into gasps and, after a few moments, Rob was silent. He leaned back and stared at Henry with pain-glazed eyes.

At first the flushed and twisted face was almost unrecognizable. Henry had seen the same look on the faces of cops who came upon victims of brutal murder, including, sometimes, their fellow officers.

"We don't know that Catherine herself is hurt, son," he said, speaking as gently as he could. "She's probably going to be naked and embarrassed when we find her, but remember the banging? If she did that, she's definitely alive."

Rob stirred, then relaxed and leaned against Henry for a tick of time before he pushed away again. "It's been over twenty-four hours since I heard the banging. She must have been alone when she did that, but later...? How many people are involved here? The man who hit me? Al? Maybe Al could have..." He ducked his head.

Henry surprised himself by wondering if Rob's father had ever hugged him. *Probably not*. Aloud he said, "It sounds like you think the person who hit you in the bluff-shelter, or maybe one of his partners, also abducted Catherine."

"Well, yes, don't you?" Rob's chin came up.

"Quite possible. Any other conclusion assumes a lot of

coincidences. That means this is looking like something way too big for us to handle alone. We should go for help."

"Oh, no, I'm not leaving, and if my only option is handling it alone, you bet I will. Just watch me. Go for help if you want, but I'm heading into that cave now." In spite of the rough floor, he began running toward the tunnel.

Caught by surprise, it took Henry several moments to catch up and grab him again. "Wait! Crashing about like a bull elephant isn't going to help Catherine. We might as well walk along this tunnel shouting, 'Hello, anybody home? Come get us.' *Do you understand me?*"

Rob hesitated, stared at Henry, then nodded, though his eyes again gleamed with pain, and—Henry thought— defiance.

"Say it," Henry whispered. "Say 'I understand.'"

Rob looked at the floor. "I understand."

"All right then, we'll keep going, but very cautiously. You can still lead since you know more about these caves than I do, but we'll be stopping every ten steps to turn off our flashlights and look and listen for light or sounds. We'll also watch for hiding places that could hold someone ready to attack us, as well as offer a place for us to hide if we need that. Do you hear me, Robert? If you don't agree, so help me I'll knock you unconscious and drag you out of here."

"Yes. Sorry. But...Catherine..."

"I know, son. And it's for her sake that we can't let our emotions overrule clear thinking. What we do from now on is important for Catherine and for us. Let's do it the best we can.

"Ready? Okay, ten steps, then stop, ten steps and stop. Keep the shovel ready in your right hand. Still got the Mace?"

Rob dug in his pocket and held it out.

"Right. Keep it in your pocket. In here, it would probably be hard to use it on someone without the chance of getting at least one of us, too. Think of that before you consider using it. The stuff is potent, and believe me, I know what I'm talking about.

"Okay, we're ready to do the first ten steps."

Catherine had her back to the tunnel, intent on finishing work at the sides of her niche. She felt so slow, but the niche was ready at last. One more yank on the boiler and...

She hadn't heard him or noticed his light.

"Well, well, so it *was* you that Blade decided to play with this time. I wondered about it when we heard a woman had gone missing and you never showed up at your tent.

"He turned out to be a real jackass. Always letting what's in his britches get the best of him. Reckon Miller an' me are better off now he's outta the way. Miller's right, he caused too many problems so..." Al made a slicing motion across his throat, "bye-bye, Blade."

His eyes dropped from her face and he seemed to notice she was nude for the first time. "But hey, I like how Blade got his playthings ready. Kinda too bad he was...interrupted.

"I guess I might say you caused his early demise. He promised there would be no more goings on, but he'd done that before, and each time he ended up with another woman. Miller said it was the last straw after Blade showed up late for our meeting. We could easy tell why, he had that look. We was in danger every time he let his women go free to talk, and when they went missing, well, y'know, it was bad for us either way. Reckon he had to be taken care of."

She shut her eyes as the flashlight gleamed over her, stopping to highlight spots he probably considered of special interest.

"Hope you ain't too cold." He began laughing, a loud, unpleasant roar of mirth. "Don't worry, I ain't going to touch you, not *that way* at least. I got control. But you musta already figured out you're a problem. I gotta get you away from here, what with treasures still to be hauled out from these caves. But...well, now, everybody knows you've gone missing, so nobody will be surprised if you turn up in one of the mines at Rush. Some of 'em I can get in, so a curious woman could too."

Catherine tried to speak, and then stopped, furious when all that came out was a croak. Did he expect her to plead for her life? She wasn't about to do it. Anyway, why would it matter? It was easy to understand what her chances were now.

She swallowed over and over, pulling imagined moisture into her mouth, and began again. "I know you from the campground. Our neighbor...the trailer...the three of us talked about Indian history. We gave you a Pepsi."

He shrugged, still laughing between his words. "Well, that's how life goes. Bummer. Camping's a pretty good cover, right? Oh, I got me a little place in Harrison, but business keeps me here at the river lots of the time. My trailer moves around easy. It's handy for short stays at different places in the park, and for tran...transporting merchandise, as Miller puts it.

"See, he likes to have his house to himself. Oh, a few times he let Blade stay over, and maybe, since Blade is gone, he'll want me there some. Closer to the action when we got big things going. I'll keep the trailer, though."

He paused to look over Catherine's head. "Hey, what you been workin' on? Well, I'll be... You find something good for us? After your boyfriend talked about Indian stuff, I kinda thought it'd be a good idea to keep an eye on the two of you." He stepped toward her.

In the background—surely hallucination—Catherine had begun hearing sounds. Bangs and shouting. Then silence. Al wasn't reacting, but he did make a lot of noise when he laughed.

"What's in that hole, girlie? Let's have a look."

Ghostly shrieks and wails began echoing along the tunnel. No way Al could miss that. He lifted his head and turned toward the sound, frozen into immobility. He seemed uncertain about what to do.

Hope had fluttered inside Catherine when she first heard the sounds, but when the wailing began and Al stopped to listen, the flutter died.

Then she heard shouting. *Rob! No, no, not now, Rob, oh, no.*

Al looked back at her. "W-e-l-l, who do ya think that is? You reckon it could it be your boyfriend? We'll see, we'll just see." He pulled a gun from under his shirt and turned toward the exit tunnel, moving cautiously, pausing to listen after every step.

NO! Catherine had no voice to call a warning and no words for a prayer, but if she moved fast enough, there might be a chance to save Rob.

She scooted inside her niche and folded into a fetal curl. It looked like everything but her left arm, still handcuffed to the boiler, would be protected if she could move back quickly.

After taking one last look inside the burial cave Rob would eventually find, she steeled herself against what was coming and stuck her right arm and both legs out of the niche. Using all the strength she had left, pushing against the bottom while she pulled on the top, Catherine tipped the boiler over. Its crash rang along the tunnel.

For a few seconds all the world's stillness gathered around her. Only cutting pain from her handcuffed wrist told her she was alive.

Al's running steps and shouting broke the silence. "What the...you *stupid*...! We put that boiler there to hold up the beam." He was screaming now. "I gotta tip it back up, help me...help me..."

Catherine folded all but her imprisoned arm back into the niche and pulled the jacket over her head just as the beam crashed down. A few rocks plicked after it in slow motion, then roaring and dust and chaotic hell filled the tunnel.

Chapter 19

OAK, HICKORY, PINE, cedar, dogwood, redbud, walnut, sassafras, sumac—and not one leaf had stirred since she came out on the porch at dawn. It was most certainly peaceful, but Carrie was in no mood for peace.

She leaned against the cabin's porch railing and turned her head back and forth, once more surveying the woodland vista. A typical Ozarks forest, but this morning it was so quiet that not a grass blade moved. Even the birds and bugs seemed awed into silence. Squirrels? Where were they? Had some evil force paralyzed the entire world while she slept?

The only motion she could identify was in the form of words bouncing inside her head, repeating what Henry said in the note she'd almost memorized by now.

Cara, my love,

Rob left the hospital on his own accord about 4:00 yesterday. He rented a small moving van (no car rentals available) and drove to Tyler Bend after sleeping several hours in a shopping center parking lot. In the meantime, the hospital traced me and phoned me here at one o'clock this morning, so I was awake and up, ready to meet him when he drove into the campground.

He said he left the hospital so he could go to Rush and locate

Catherine. He insists he knows where she is.

I couldn't let him go alone, therefore, by the time you read this, the two of us will be somewhere beyond Rush, probably in the cave Rob says he can find without climbing back up to the bluffshelter. I hope either we, or the search team, will have located Catherine by the time you wake up.

He says the cave that opens at the back of the shelter he was marooned in must have one or more other entrances. It's his belief that Catherine used (or was forced to use) one of the openings near ground level, and she's in the cave system somewhere— because of the banging sounds you already know about.

I hope he's right, she is in there and is okay. But be prepared, something may have gone terribly wrong. Otherwise, why hasn't she found her way out by now?

Rob says cell phones don't work around most of Rush, and I know they don't work in caves, but I'll call you as soon as I can.

Pray for all of us. I love you, Henry

P.S. Rob borrowed your 'C. C. McCrite' credit card and twenty dollars. He took them from your purse at the hospital. He says to tell you he's sorry, but he had to have money, and he'll pay you back for everything.

"Drat!" she told the silent world. She'd been left out— again!—and though it wasn't anyone's fault, especially not Henry's, she felt both helpless and useless. It had been several months since she and Henry, not to mention she, Eleanor, and Shirley, had any real detecting work to do, and she'd missed the action. Now a huge problem faced all of them, her family was in need, possibly in danger, while she stood on a quiet porch looking at trees.

"Drat," she said again.

"How's that?" said Shirley as she let the screen door creak shut and, holding a full coffee cup, came to sit on the porch swing.

"Oh, well, it's too quiet, that's all."

"Huh, this quiet stuff is fine with me. I don't know about you, but I could get downright lazy here. I can't remember when I've slept beyond dawn, and this morning I came downstairs past that to find you'd already made my coffee. Whooee, I might not go home tomorrow after all." She paused to sip coffee, then pushed a foot against the floor, starting the swing's lazy back and forth motion.

"So, what's that paper, if I'm not being too nosy?"

Carrie went to the swing and handed the note to Shirley, but didn't sit down. She was afraid a new landing on the wooden slats would splash coffee.

Shirley reached over to put her mug on the porch floor, then spread the note on her lap. Relieved of worry over a spill, Carrie sat beside her.

As Shirley's fingers traced the lines, Carrie remembered that her friend once admitted she hadn't been able to read until after her first child started school. Then, shamed by the fact that she couldn't make sense of her daughter's schoolwork, she enrolled at the literacy council in town and worked with a tutor there until she could read her children's school work, the newspaper, and the Bible. Some people's handwriting was still difficult for her, though.

Shirley held the paper toward her. "What's this word?"

"Access. Umm, it is hard to read that, isn't it? Henry sort of slips over the letter C in his writing. Almost looks like 'asses.' It means... well, it's something that lets you into something else. Oh, dear, I'm not putting it right—I wish I had a dictionary here. It's like a door into the cave he's talking about. A door gives you access to a room."

"Access. I think I've got it. So there's another opening into the cave, Rob says, and Catherine maybe went in that way? Then she got stuck or something?"

"Yes, exactly."

Shirley finished reading the note, handed it back to Carrie and stood. "So, how about we eat some cereal? Then after, maybe we'll put on our hiking boots and drive toward Rush. On the map it looks to be about an hour from here. We could pack a lunch. For five?"

Shirley still hadn't picked up her coffee mug, so Carrie stood too and hugged her friend.

"Gosh, it sure *is* a ghost town," Carrie said as Shirley drove into Rush. "Those houses look wretched. But they do have a lot of...atmosphere."

"Don't want Disneyland in a place like this," Shirley said. "Guess the buildings are okay as long as park folks keep what's left standing." She slowed the car. "Now, whereabouts do you suppose we should start looking for Henry and Rob?"

"Rob talked about seeing concrete piers left from an old processing mill. He and Catherine walked up a trail beginning there, and he hiked along the base of a bluff until he found the rock shelter. Oh, hey, there's Catherine's red Jeep in that parking lot."

Shirley pulled into the lot and stopped her car while they both stared at the Jeep. "Looks okay," she said, "I suppose it's locked."

A pickup truck came in behind them and, without honking, circled awkwardly around to park beside the Jeep. Two men got out. They both wore shoes and pants that looked ready for heavy outdoor work. Badges and insignia on their neat shirts and caps identified them as park personnel. Both men ignored the Jeep, but the elder of the two shouldered a backpack and walked toward the Cadillac.

"I'll bet they're getting ready to go searching for Catherine," Carrie said. "They didn't even glance at her Jeep. I think they know who it belongs to and have already looked it over. Do we tell them why we're here?"

"Hunh-unh, let's wait on that. We don't know the lay of the land yet." Shirley rolled down her window. "Hello, officer," she said, "we're just looking around. Sorry if my car was in your way."

"It's fine. You can pull in and park on the other side of us if you like, there's plenty of room today. Glad you're here to enjoy the Buffalo National River. Anything we can do to help you?"

"I don't think so. We plan to do a bit of hiking, and we brought a picnic lunch. Oh, you know, you *could* tell me something. A friend said there's a trail starting near concrete work left from an old ore processing mill. Do you know where that is?"

The man pointed. "Along the road. You can't miss it, it's an easy walk." He touched the bill of his ball cap. "Nice day for a picnic, ladies. I'm sure you'll pick up any wrappings or picnic leftovers. The picnic area and trash containers are behind you across the road. There are pit toilets there, too. If you're hiking, stay in the park boundaries. There's been a little drug activity outside the park."

"Thanks," Shirley said. She shut her window, then pulled into the parking space indicated.

Carrie unfastened her seat belt. "Are we really going to take all the food we brought with us? Those men headed off in the same direction they pointed out for us, but they're moving pretty fast. They won't be around to see whether we carry enough for a picnic or not."

"I think we should take it all," Shirley said. "Our guys will be hungry unless they thought to bring food, which I doubt. Besides, we don't know how far it is to get to them,

it might be a while." She went around the car, opened the
trunk, and pulled out two large canvas bags with strap handles. "Here, take one of these. They'll hold most of what's
in the picnic cooler. They won't be bad to carry, you'll see. I
tote groceries in them all the time."

They divided plates, cups, and plastic utensils, then
began on the food. When Shirley got to the bottles of juice
Carrie said, "Let's leave all but the water, I think the liquids
are heaviest." Shirley put the juice back in the cooler and
handed Carrie a large bottle of water, taking one for herself.
"Hope we brought enough," she said. "If they've got Catherine, she'll sure be thirsty."

Carrie wiggled the water bottle into her tote and—
ashamed—said she could handle a bottle of juice too. She
said no more about what she did or didn't want to carry, and
remained silent while Shirley tucked a worn print tablecloth
over the contents of her bag.

"Ready?" Shirley asked.

"Let's visit the pit toilet first," Carrie said. "Then I'm
ready."

After finding the concrete piers and rental truck, they
chugged along an increasingly difficult trail for what seemed
a long time. Carrie had begun shifting the food tote from
one shoulder to another every few minutes when they came
to a clearing with a flat rock that looked perfect for sitting.
She sank onto the cool surface and gladly dropped the bag
beside her. "How about a drink?"

Shirley pulled out two cups and held them while Carrie
poured. "Guess a whole lotta people stop here to rest," she
said. "See, the grass is mashed."

"Everyone's been careful not to walk on those pretty
white flowers though," Carrie said, finishing her water. "Rue

anemone, one of my favorites. See, the opening buds look pale lavender." She glanced around. "It's beautiful here, but we'd better move on. The guys are ahead of us by several hours."

They hiked in silence for a while. In spite of concern over the problems that brought her here, Carrie realized she was enjoying the landscape. It was more rugged than the hills and hollows around her home at Blackberry Hollow, and that made it interesting. There was a real joy in seeing so many wildflowers, new kinds of growing things, the rugged bluffs, and the river itself. She wondered if Shirley was enjoying it too.

"Pretty here," she said.

"Yup, all kinds of flowers. I've never figured out how some of them grow in what looks like nothing but rocks. Do that at home, too, and I notice we get more flowers when the spring is wet like this one has been."

"Right." After a short silence, Carrie said, "You know, I'm sorry now that I didn't come on this trip with Henry and the kids from the beginning. He did offer to get a cabin after I...well, after I said I wouldn't sleep in a tent."

"Umm," Shirley said.

"I suppose I should have done it just because I love him and it's something he enjoys."

"Well, now, marrying a man doesn't mean you have to be all eat up by him and his wishes, especially if you've been used to doing things on your own. But you can bend sometimes, and so can he. Being married means doing a bit of bending, but not so far anything breaks. I'm sure the both of you know that."

"Yes, and that's a good way to put it...bending," Carrie said. "When I think about it, I see Henry's done most of the bending and I feel like a creep. You know, I preached to Rob

about unselfishness being a part of love. I've been thinking about that, and how maybe I really should have been
preaching to myself. Rob kept telling me he was too focused
on his own interests when he hiked off and left Catherine.
Am I any better?"

"Don't beat up on yourself. Life gives us bumps, makes
us grow. You and Henry had plenty of that in years past.
By now the both of you know you can get over the bumps,
learn from them, and maybe go ahead a little different way.
All of us, including the two of you, can tell you're happy
together. Move on, forget about what happened last week or
last month or whenever. Just grow out of it."

Carrie said simply, "Thanks for being such a good
friend, Shirley. Don't know how I got so lucky."

"Shoot," said Shirley, and they continued picking their
way along the base of the bluff in silence.

Then, in the midst of thinking she might like to learn
more about fishing, Carrie felt the ground tremble under
her feet. "Ooops, did I imagine that?"

"No, ma'am, the ground shook, I felt it. You suppose the
New Madrid has cut loose again after all these years?"

"I..." There was another shake and a noise that sounded
like a muffled landslide. Carrie looked up. Nothing was
happening above them. "Shirley, that noise must be coming
from behind this rock wall. Something is breaking up inside
there. Do you think it's going to collapse?"

Shirley was no longer beside her. "I can't say," she
shouted from a stand of river cane several yards distant, "but
you'd best get away from under that bluff right quick."

Carrie hurried toward Shirley; shielded by the stand
of cane, they both turned to look back. A few small rocks
bounced down the bluff and, while they stared, a cloud of
dust exploded from its base.

Neither of them spoke until after the noise stopped and the dust settled. There was one last feeble *plick* from a falling pebble, then silence.

"What happened?" Carrie said, surveying the landscape. "That was awful, but you know, everything looks about the same as before."

"Hunh, it was scary enough while it lasted. Where did the dust come from?"

The two of them stepped cautiously toward the bluff face.

Finally Shirley said, "My stars, there's a hole in the bluff. Was it there before? I bet that's where the dust came from."

"I didn't notice a hole," Carrie said, "but I couldn't swear it wasn't there. Maybe some of the rocks that fell were covering it." She stood on tiptoe to look in. "Wish we had a flashlight."

"You aren't thinking you'll go in there!"

"Oh, no, just curious. There's a big space behind the hole. I wish I could see in."

"Leave it alone, I say, who knows what might happen next. I guess we had us a little bitty earthquake. I wonder, are we the only ones who felt it?"

First there was an echoing *clang,* and both Rob and Henry stopped moving forward. Then they heard Al's shouts, followed almost immediately by a roar and a wall of choking dust.

They'd just left the cave tunnel and were five steps into what Rob had identified as a mine shaft when the horrifying noises began. Rob jerked back, stumbled against Henry, then both of them turned and ran like creatures with a devil on their tails. They didn't stop until they reached the garage.

Rob leaned against the wall, gasping. "It can't be, it just

can't, can't, *can't*!"

Henry, slightly less distraught, stared around the garage. How long had they been in that cave? It was now full daylight...and the Thunderbird had gone.

Chapter 20

THE WOMEN TRUDGED on in silence. Shirley seemed preoccupied. Carrie was simply occupied in doing battle with her imagination.

Lord, give me strength, she thought, and meant it literally. She shifted the heavy food tote again and began saying Bible verses to herself, trying to blot out increasing worry about Catherine and how the peculiar earthquake might have affected her safety.

Finally Shirley said, "I've been thinking...trying to figure out how Catherine could stay so lost. I only saw her that once, at your wedding, but she seemed a bright sort of woman, and she's built sturdy. I don't see her going off inside a cave or mine on her own. Could someone have...well, you know, kidnapped her, or something like? I don't want to draw doom down, but..." She stopped walking and turned to face Carrie. "I wouldn't be honest if I didn't tell you I'm fearful."

Heat flamed in Carrie's face. If calm, wise Shirley thought the worst...well, she couldn't stand it, she just couldn't.

"No!" was all she managed at first, and it was almost a

shout. After a moment, she said, more calmly, "Sorry. I'm having a hard time with imagining awful things myself. They just won't stop coming. Now I'm saying parts of the 91st Psalm, over and over, and that helps. I've been saying it like this, '*She* that dwelleth in the secret place of the most High shall abide under the shadow of the Almighty.'"

"Keep doing it," Shirley said, "and I will too."

Carrie was up to "For he shall give his angels charge over thee" for the third time when Shirley glimpsed the clearing and put out a hand to stop her. They both slid forward until, partially hidden by underbrush, they could see the open area clearly. "A house, a garage, four men," Shirley said, "including Rob and Henry."

But Carrie had already seen her husband and son, dropped her tote bag, and was in the clearing, running. She banged into Henry's chest with an audible *whump,* raising dust from his filthy shirt. At the same instant she reached a hand toward her son, trying to hug them both. "Have you found...?" she began as soon as she could speak.

"No, little love. Instead, our problems have increased fourfold." He ran his hand over her hair for a minute, then pulled back. "There's a cave opening behind the garage over there. Rob and I went in and hadn't gone too far when we saw that those digging a mine shaft years ago broke into the cave tunnel. Just as we were entering the mine, sounds of rock falling began, and we soon figured out the mine ceiling was collapsing somewhere ahead of us. We think human action may have triggered it because, just before the collapse began, Rob and I agree we heard something that sounded like a large metal object banging against rock. We also heard a man shouting."

"But not Catherine?"

"Not Catherine."

By then Shirley was with them, awkwardly patting Rob on the shoulder, and grasping Henry's arm.

"We're radioing for help," a voice behind Henry said.

Carrie turned her head and recognized the two rangers from the parking lot. Henry held an arm toward the man who had spoken, the elder of the two. "Ranger Clyde Dunn, and," he indicated the second man, "Ranger Bill Jankowitz. My wife, Carrie McCrite, and our friend, Shirley Booth."

Ranger Dunn put a walkie-talkie about the size of a chunky TV remote into a holder on his belt, and said, "Hello again," to Carrie and Shirley before going on. "I talked to Buffalo Point. They're sending tools, as much of the staff as they can muster, and maintenance will bring a small loader. I think we can get it in the mine to move the heaviest rocks out. I also asked them to notify the Sheriff's department and call our staff archeologist, Dr. Fletcher, since you saw those things in the trunk of the missing car. They'll send an ambulance as well. Now, until everyone gets here..."

"We wait," Henry finished for him.

"More or less. Our truck is in the parking lot at Rush, and I'm going back to bring it here on that road leading to the house. Under the circumstances we'll ignore the *Keep Out* signs. We need the truck because all rangers here are trained EMTs and carry medical supplies in their vehicles. Bill's going down to watch the private road in case the car you saw—or another one—comes back."

He gestured toward the house. "Did you find anything helpful in there?"

Rob spoke up. "No, it's just a...house. Looks like one occupant, a man, and the place is so clean a housekeeping service could be coming every day. No sign of archeological items, no sign of Catherine."

"Of course we were anxious to learn if Catherine was being held in there," Henry said. "When there was no answer to repeated knocking and shouting, we felt breaking in was justified."

"Understood," said Dunn, as he walked away.

"So now you're sure Catherine is in that mine?" Shirley asked.

Rob looked at his mom, then at Shirley. "Come with me," he said, "I'll show you."

When they entered the cave, Rob pointed mutely to the bits of fabric on the floor. The two women stared, processing what they were seeing. Finally Shirley said, "Oh, dear heaven."

"Catherine's clothing?" Carrie asked, and Rob nodded as she looked past him into the tunnel. "Where's the cave-in? Do you think more will fall?"

"Nothing in the cave system itself is unstable so far as we can tell. The rangers looked around in here and agree the collapse was entirely in the mine, the cave is okay. But we have no way of knowing how much of the mine was affected."

"They plan to dig through?"

"Yes."

"Can we go see where the collapse is?"

"Not me," Shirley said. "Leave me out of crawling through tunnels."

"The cave tunnel is open, and easy to walk through, at least the part where we were. It's only the mine that's full of rock to about three-fourths of the way up."

"Why can't you crawl over?"

"The rock is too unstable. The rangers advised against it. They said we might cause rock slides, do even more harm to...anyone trapped there, let alone endanger ourselves.

The workers will shore up the walls and ceiling as they dig through."

"Show me the place," Carrie said firmly, and, in a moment, Rob nodded.

"Y'all be careful," Shirley said as she sat down on a wooden crate at the edge of the cave opening.

They'd walked several yards when Carrie asked, "What made this tunnel? It wasn't water, I'm walking in dust."

"Not all Ozarks caves are wet today, but that doesn't mean they weren't water-formed, aided by shifts in the land over millions of years. You already know underground topography in the Ozarks isn't often solid rock; there are many cracks and faults. Sometime during the last ten million years or so, rain seeps gathered here. The weak carbonic acid in rain water was increased by what it picked up on and in the ground. That water made its way through wherever it could, and ate at underlying dolomite and limestone. The flow of underground water—everything from small drips to big rivers—shaped these tunnels, and of course that's still happening many places in the Ozarks."

"Well, it's sure dry now."

"The water table is much lower today, and I guess the rock arrangement above us is conformed to shut out seeps. But this cave isn't unique; they've discovered around two hundred and seventy-five of them at the National River so far, both wet and dry. It's not all that different from the area around you at Walden Valley."

Carrie remembered when she, Henry, and his daughter Susan had been trapped in a Walden Valley cave by a killer with a high-powered rifle, and said simply, "I know."

Rob stopped walking. "Here we are."

The sinuous curves and unique forms of the cave tunnel ended abruptly, intersected by plainer and rougher rock walls. Rob pointed his flashlight down the mine tunnel, revealing a pile of loose rock, some of it in chunks half as large as Carrie.

She stood in silence for a few minutes, thinking.

"Rob, when Shirley and I were walking along the base of the bluff, at one point we felt the ground shake. A few rocks fell, and then a puff of dust blew out from the bluff face. When things quieted down, we went to see where the dust came from. There was a hole we hadn't seen before. It was partially concealed by river cane, but we thought maybe rocks broken loose by the earthquake, as we called it, had fallen away, exposing the hole. I don't have a flashlight with me but I looked in best I could, and I think there's a cave room just beyond the bluff face. Do you suppose...?" She stopped.

Rob stared at her, frowning.

In the silence, they both heard something. A soft *bang-bang-bang, bang-bang-bang,* echoing over the wall of rock. At first neither of them said anything, just listened, frozen.

Then Rob began shouting. "Catherine, Catherine, hang on, I'm coming! Hang on, Catherine, hang on."

Chapter 21

H ANG ON, CATHERINE, hang on. I'm coming!"
Rob's shout was answered by two faint bangs, then
silence. He began scrambling up the pile of rock but was defeated when he set off a slide, tumbling him back to the cave
floor and sending one large rock rolling toward his mother.
She jumped sideways, wondering if his resulting shout was a
form of apology or simply vocalized despair.

"Wait, son. What about that opening in the bluff face
Shirley and I saw? Remember the dust cloud? Couldn't we
go look through the hole, see if maybe we can get to Catherine that way? I think..."

He was already jogging toward the opening of the cave.

When they reached the entry Shirley was no longer
there, and Rob yanked the lid off the crate she'd been sitting
on.

"I think there are tools in here, we can...handcuffs?
What are those doing in a tool box?"

Shirley poked her head through the back door of the
garage. "I've got lunch ready out here, come grab a bite."

Rob jumped like a skittish horse and dropped the geologist's pick he'd just pulled out of the box. Carrie grabbed it

from the floor as she said, "Thanks, Shirley, in a minute."

"Mom..."

"We need to eat something," she said firmly, "we can get a sandwich and head for that opening while the others begin work in the mine. I think we want to start this side project on our own—see if it's a wild goose chase or not. Besides, everyone else has a big enough job here."

After hesitating a moment he nodded, and they went to join the others. Rob told Henry he'd heard more banging, so Catherine must be alive, but unable to get out. "We've gotta be so careful going in," he said. "The rangers were right about unstable rock; I tried to climb over and started a landslide. I'm afraid we might crush her."

Now Henry ate more rapidly and without conversation, as if intent only on starting work. Rob found one of Shirley's empty tote bags and went back into the cave to load it with tools.

Shirley and Carrie were getting ready to unwrap their sandwiches when noises outside the garage announced the arrival of workers and equipment. Shirley shooed Henry out just as Rob returned with the tote bag and Henry's back-pack. Carrie picked up the other tote, dropped in a still full water bottle, then began wrapping bits of food she thought Catherine might be able to eat easily—plain bread, a slice of cheese, some milk chocolate.

"What's that for?" Shirley asked. "You've got a sandwich, and here are cookies. You don't need..."

"Shhh," Carrie said. "We're going back to the hole you and I found. Since we saw dust, it has to be connected to the tunnel cave-in somehow. We'll look for Catherine there while they begin clearing at this end. There's nothing you and I can do here anyway, and Rob agrees looking in that opening is worth a try."

"Oh...I see what you're about. Well, now, I'd best go along and stay outside so you have some back-up if you need it. Where're you gonna get flashlights?"

"Mine is in this backpack," Rob said, "and Henry left his over there with his jacket. I imagine the rangers brought lights, so I don't mind borrowing his." He flushed and looked at his mother. "About that money and the credit card I borrowed..."

She fluttered a hand at him. "Never mind, I understand. We'll talk about it later."

She found Henry helping unload shovels and picks from the back of a truck and told him she and Shirley were going for a walk and quiet time to pray. Then she waved an arm vaguely behind her and added that Rob was meeting up with more workers "out there." All this earned her a quick cheek kiss and a distracted nod, with the admonition, "Be careful, and stay within shouting distance."

Shielded by trees, she, Rob, and Shirley hurried back along the base of the bluff, sandwiches in hand.

Carrie had the food tote, covered by the worn tablecloth she'd put in after remembering Catherine was probably naked. The tablecloth could serve as a wrap. Rob carried the tool sack, as well as his backpack with first aid supplies and the flashlights. Shirley, walking stick in hand, led the way.

Carrie was still fighting awful imaginings, including the possibility of rape, which had shot into top concern when she saw the shredded clothing. And there were all the other darkly menacing *What if*s, not to mention the large possibility the hole might not lead them to Catherine at all. But then, anything was better than waiting on the sidelines while a bunch of people dug at tons of rock and the loader scooped it out of the tunnel. She hadn't lied to Henry; she did need this time for prayer.

Ten minutes later the three of them stood at the opening into the bluff. Rob bent to look at the detritus on the ground below the hole. "Odd," he said, "it's almost like bits of fired clay. I wouldn't expect to find that here. Looks like someone covered this hole on purpose." He rubbed a pinch of the material between his fingers and said, "Fired clay with burned shell in it?" as if talking to himself. "Maybe shell helps keep it from shrinking."

To Carrie, it looked like rusty concrete bits.

Ground inspection finished, Rob poked his head and the arm holding a flashlight through the hole. He stayed that way for so long that his mother finally tapped his shoulder. "What do you see?"

He waved his free arm impatiently and stayed where he was while Carrie fidgeted and Shirley brushed off a rock to sit on.

Finally Rob pulled out of the opening. "I can't believe it. Looks like we've found archeological treasure. If it weren't for Catherine, I wouldn't think of going in there and disturbing what I see. Everything's dust-covered but I can identify pottery, tools, mesh bags holding something roundish, maybe nuts. There's what may be items of clothing—animal skins, coarse fabric. It's like people centuries ago closed the door to their storage room, went on a journey, and... never came back."

He rubbed his forehead and stared at the ground.

"Shirley, that ranger said he'd called for the staff archeologist, Dr. Anderson Fletcher, to come—you know, because of the stuff we saw in the trunk of the Thunderbird and the good chance it came from that cave. Would you go back and see if he's arrived yet? Bring him here quietly, if you can. If he hasn't come, wait, and then get him here as soon as possible."

Carrie said angrily, "Are you forgetting Catherine? I don't care *what's* in there, she's our priority."

"I know that, Mom. While Shirley goes for Dr. Fletcher, I'm going in the cave."

As he started to swing himself up into the opening, she said, "Hold it. You come back down here and boost me first. You are not going in alone."

She ignored Rob's resentful look as well as the rough shove administered to her rear end as she lurched over the wall and into the cave. The two tote bags and backpack came through the hole next, then Rob joined her. She barely glanced at objects scattered about the floor and, to his credit, Rob now ignored them too. He immediately began sweeping the cave walls with his flashlight.

"I don't see an opening yet. Take this flashlight and go around that way, looking at both the walls and floor. I'll start here and go the opposite direction. Don't step on anything on the floor if you can help it, and don't make any more footprints than you have to. Search the floor first to be sure you aren't disturbing any old footprints or other mark-ings, though the new dust cloud possibly erased what might have been here earlier."

Carrie obeyed, and in only a minute she said, "Hey, this slab of rock must conceal an opening. I can feel cold air coming over it. It's sealed with more of that mud plaster like you saw outside, but an area at the top has broken open. The pieces from that crunch under my feet. The stones have black marks, like a fire was built here."

Rob's flashlight joined hers, surveying the plastered rock. "My gosh, maybe they put clay around the rock to seal the opening, then burned wood to harden the clay. But they'd have had to do it some special way, or even more than once, since clay shrinks when it dries." He took out the geologist's pick. "Well, here goes. Stand back in case that rock comes down." Chips of clay flew, and in a few minutes the rock stood alone.

"Are we strong enough to move it?" Carrie asked.

"Maybe. It's kind of like a sliding door. If I can just..." He shoved, but the rock didn't move. Carrie pushed with him, but the rock stayed where it was.

"We need a lever," he said. "What can we use?" He looked in the tool bag. "The tire tool, if it's strong enough. Keep away."

He wedged the pry bar end of the tool under the rock and pushed. Again Carrie joined him and put her hands over his. Together they pushed.

"*Back*," he shouted as the huge block of stone, instead of sliding sideways, tilted away from the opening and, with a tremendous *thunk*, fell to the floor.

"I didn't have time to look," Rob said while they were waiting for the dust to settle. "Is there anything under where the rock fell?"

Carrie cautiously opened her eyes, took her hand away from her nose, coughed, spit dirt. "I, uh, don't think so." At the moment she didn't really care.

Rob led the way through the opening. They were in a cave tunnel not unlike the one they'd entered behind the garage, but more irregular. Forward progress was challenged by rocky outcrops and narrow passages that barely gave them room to squeeze through. Once they had to get on their hands and knees and inch along, snake-like—an awkward process since both were tugging tote bags and carrying flashlights.

"Looks like this passage is ending," Carrie said as she turned sideways to get through a narrow opening and wished she'd skipped lunch.

"No, not yet." Rob's flashlight played over the walls as they made their way along.

Carrie surveyed the bottom of the tunnel. "Lots of dust on the floor and caught in some of the rougher wall places," she said, brushing at the dust on her jeans.

"Um-hm, and it looks like there are sealed-off side tunnels or rooms along here. I've counted three so far. But I don't think any of those lead to Catherine. The sealed openings look intact. We need to find a place where dust got through."

"I feel air moving against my face."

After another few minutes of inching their way forward, Rob's roaming flashlight stopped, spotlighting an opening above them. "Hey, Mom, here's a place dust could get through." He ran a finger along the ledge below the opening. "There's dust on this ledge, a lot of it, and broken bits of clay. It looks like the force of the mine collapse pushed this stuff out. I'm going up there and take a look."

Helped by Carrie, he climbed until he could stand on the ledge. Though he stretched up as far as possible, his head didn't reach the opening. "I can't see in yet, it's too far above me. Hand me the geologist's pick and stand back. I'll make the hole larger."

Carrie obediently stood out of the way while pieces of clay flew. Finally Rob said, "Looks like it's going to be a real doorway."

When the opening was large enough he poked his head and flashlight arm through. Carrie endured his silence for only a moment before she asked, "What do you see?"

He pulled back, banging his head on the side of the opening in the process. "There's another room here for Dr. Fletcher. It's full of..." He stopped.

Carrie didn't ask "full of what?" because they both saw a

light in the tunnel. Rob called, "Dr. Fletcher? Shirley?"

There was no answer, but the light brightened as it came closer. Carrie said, "Dr. Fletcher, we're here," knowing full well Shirley wouldn't willingly come into a cave.

They couldn't see who held the light because of the glare, but in a minute, and before she could react, a man was with them, his arm circling her neck. His flashlight bumped her chin as he twisted her around to face the ledge. At the same instant she felt the hard push of what had to be a gun barrel against her side.

"Easy now, young man. Drop that pick and put your hands up. Back away from the hole slowly, then turn and sit on the ledge facing your mother. I have a gun on her, so no funny business. Keep your hands where I can see them or...I'll shoot." He hesitated as if figuring out what to say next, then added, "Shoot to kill."

Carrie felt like she'd entered a fantasy world where one disaster after another rushed at her. *Fantasy, yes. The man sounds like he's playing tough guy on a television crime show.*

The gun poked her side again. That was no fantasy.

Chapter 22

RINGING? SOMEWHERE between her eyes a bell
rang: *Bong...bong...bong.*

Rob? Was he banging on the tank to say he'd come?
"Rob? Are you here?" Her unanswered whisper sounded in
the tunnel, wavering between tumbled rocks. The merci-
less gong continued, swallowing the whisper—fading in
and out—beating a rhythm to accompany pain throbbing
behind her eyes.

Catherine wiggled the fingers on her left hand, then,
remembering, tensed her arm and tugged. The sharp grab of
metal on her wrist stopped motion, and a wounded animal
whimper vibrated from somewhere below the gong. The
pipe had not broken loose after all.

She laid her head back against the niche wall. At least
she'd stopped Al. She'd heard him yell as the rocks and dirt
came down. He'd had a gun, but she had stopped him from
getting to Rob. A sigh flickered after the thin whimper.

Rest now. She could rest.

Catherine was silent only a moment before she stirred,
lifted her head again. No, no, not rest. She really had heard
his voice. It couldn't have been hallucination. Rob...Rob...

maybe, if she banged a signal...

Catherine's right hand lifted, her palm skimmed over rocks, finally closing around one. She reached out, following the pain in her wrist toward the tank. Then she banged, the familiar sequence of three, keeping time with the pain inside her head.

The noise sounded so faint now. Would it be heard? Bang harder, she had to try harder. But she couldn't do it, she couldn't.

Catherine shut her eyes, drew her arm back, and rested again. Then, out of a dream, she heard: "Hang on, Catherine, hang on. I'm coming."

Ahhhh, Rob. Now she could sleep. He was all right, and he'd said he was coming.

Henry noticed that Rob was with Carrie and Shirley when they walked away from the clearing, and a twinge of worry pulled at him. He stopped in mid-stride as he carried tools toward the open garage door, staring after the three. Not only did calmly leaving a scene of action seem out of character for his wife, Rob had been frantically intent on getting through the tunnel to Catherine. What was up?

For a moment he thought he'd follow them, but just then Clyde Dunn shouted that they were ready to begin clearing the tunnel. Henry turned back, shoving aside misgivings about the defections of his family and Shirley.

Dunn directed the work, leading the way himself. He organized workers behind him, some pulling rock away with picks or gloved hands and loading them into wheelbarrows, leaving the largest pieces for the loader. Men with lumber came next, shoving in sheets of heavy plywood braced with four-by-fours when the tunnel ceiling or walls looked unable to sustain their integrity.

Henry was working close to Dunn, lifting medium-sized rocks into a wheelbarrow, when he heard the ranger grunt in surprise. Looking up, Henry saw a human face caught in the light from Dunn's miner's cap. He stopped motion and went to the ranger's side, helping him lift boards and rocks off the twisted form. It was Al, and his hand still held a gun.

"I suppose he's dead," Dunn said. "Can you get word back to the medical team? Ask them to bring a stretcher."

"Sure, but I thought I saw a gasp of air move the dust on his face. He may be alive. Just in case, get that gun away from him, but be careful of fingerprints."

"I hear you. Tell the sheriff and the medical team what you observed," Dunn said as he bent over the man, feeling for a pulse. "I'll stay here."

I'm glad that Carrie is away from all this, Henry thought. *Rob too, for that matter. Will Catherine be in the same state as Al when we reach her?*

The man with the gun tightened his arm around Carrie's neck, yanking her up on tiptoe. "Hurry up," he said to Rob, his voice loud in Carrie's ear. "Turn around and sit on the ledge facing me. Keep your hands where I can see them."

For a moment Rob held his hands up in the classic *you've got the drop on me* pose. Then he turned very slowly, and, more casually than Carrie thought the situation warranted, sat down, dropping his arms to brace himself, then dangling his feet over the ledge. "You won't shoot us," he said, folding his hands in his lap and looking steadily toward the man with the gun.

"You think not?" the deep voice said in Carrie's ear.

"I think not."

Making each movement slow and deliberate, Rob held a hand in front of his face and put up one finger. "First, as you probably know, armed rangers and sheriff's deputies are all over this area, working to free one or two people trapped in the old mine shaft. I believe that's just behind me as I sit on this ledge. They're close enough now to hear a shot, and the sound will be amplified by the cave itself. Being in this cave isn't like being out in the open, you can't just run away in whatever direction you choose. You know what it was like getting in here.

"Second." Rob held up another finger. "Vibrations set off by a gunshot could very well bring more of the mine ceiling down, or even part of a cave tunnel, endangering everyone in here, including you. Besides that, the contained noise could damage your eardrums.

"Third." The next finger went up. "You don't seem the type of man who'd shoot a defenseless old lady who can't possibly harm you. She hasn't even seen your face. And neither of us is armed."

Carrie decided she'd forgive her son for calling her a defenseless old lady. She was too surprised by his cool behavior to take much notice anyway. He had an ulterior motive, otherwise he wouldn't dare...

Ulterior motive. Hmmm. What on earth? Seeing Rob like this opened a whole new world of ideas about her son. Was he being incredibly smart or incredibly foolish? Whichever it was, she'd find a way to praise his cool handling of their current problem. She'd do it later, of course, after whatever was going to happen—happened. *After...*

"So," Rob continued, "I suggest you simply back away from Mom, then the two of us will sit here quietly while you disappear from the cave. I suspect you already have your car parked around here somewhere, and that it's full of loot from this cave. You already know rangers and sheriff's deputies are at your house. That is your house in the clearing, isn't it? Cut your losses and leave. Take a vacation. While you're gone, sell your treasures, ditch the car, report it stolen, then come back, free as a bird."

The man flinched when Rob said, "ditch the car." He started to say something, but Rob, who had been staring at him and probably noticed the flinch, talked over his beginning protest.

"If the guy named Al that my girlfriend and I met in the Tyler Bend campground is a friend of yours, you can always blame anything illegal on him. I doubt he'll be able to argue back, since I think he was in the mine shaft when the ceiling collapsed."

Carrie heard the emotional break in Rob's words, but the man didn't seem to notice.

"Even if he survived, whatever story he gives isn't going to sound very credible. Are his fingerprints on your car?"

A gruff *Yeah* came from behind Carrie. The voice sounded less forceful now, and the gun wobbled against her side.

"Well, there you are. You can say he stole your car and whatever was in it belonged to him. You know nothing about it. That way they'll give the car back to you after they're through using it as evidence. I know your house is clean. You left the window on the porch unlocked and I went in to search, thinking my missing girlfriend might be inside."

The man behind Carrie was silent for several moments which, she thought, had to be hopeful. He must actually be thinking over Rob's suggestions. She wondered if he'd put enough facts together to realize how full of holes Rob's story was. For one thing, he hadn't asked yet how Rob knew about the car and the treasures it held. And, how *did* Rob guess it was his car...or his house, for that matter?

"You've seen me," her captor said finally.

"No. You're shining a flashlight in my face."

More silence. They began hearing a rumble through the cave walls.

"What's that?" the man said, turning toward the sound and relaxing his hold on her neck.

"They're clearing out the mine cave-in with a Bobcat loader."

Rob lifted his eyes for a second, staring over Carrie's head. Then he quickly dropped back into his conversational mode and began talking loudly, as if he were trying to drown out the rumble. "Mom and I don't care about your business. We're just here to try and find my girlfriend—the other person caught in the cave-in."

Carrie listened, astounded, while Rob babbled on and on, telling an increasingly fanciful story about how he'd gone in the mine searching for his girlfriend, heard her crying, heard the collapse start, heard the shouting of someone whose voice sounded like Al, the man camped next to them at Tyler Bend who'd said he was in the antiquities business.

At this, Carrie's captor swore. His grasp on her neck tightened again, but his arm began shaking and the gun rocked wildly.

Why is Rob keeping on with his chatter? I wish I could signal him that this man is losing patience.

The man's arm was shaking so badly he might shoot her without meaning to. She'd been thinking frantically about how to free herself, but decided she didn't dare try. Like Rob said, escaping from danger in a cave wasn't at all like running away in the open, and this man's agitation scared her anyway. *God, help us, help all of us know the right thing to do.*

Rob's voice rose even higher, almost shouting about an escape plan.

A frantic jerk almost yanked Carrie off her feet. "Shut

up, you. I'm leaving, okay? But I'm taking this woman with me to make sure you don't follow or pull some trick. You hear? If you want to see her alive, if anyone does, they'd better stay away. If no one is around to bother me, I'll let her go when I get to my car. If anyone comes after me, she goes in the car and we drive off together."

Chapter 23

ROB'S STUNNED LOOK matched Carrie's panic. The man still had a tight hold on her neck, but he'd begun waving his gun arm in the air. Following up on his words he began backing away, pulling her after him.

"Don't you move from where you are, you hear? I'll have my gun pointed at your mom the entire time, and the minute I hear or feel anything from you, I shoot her. You got that?"

A much subdued Rob nodded as Carrie and her captor moved out of his sight.

How's this guy going to get me through all these tunnels and still hold a gun? Carrie wondered as he gripped her arm and ordered her to slide ahead of him through the slit tunnel. *When we get to the tunnel where we need to crawl, maybe I can get away somehow, maybe kick him. I'm not going along easily.*

But she soon learned that defiance wasn't that big on her list when someone else held the gun. When they reached the chute tunnel, the man took his arm away from her neck and said, "Okay, lady, down on your belly. Crawl ahead of me. I'll have my hand on your ankle, and you can help pull me through. When you get to the other side, lie still on the ground. If you don't, you'll have a bullet hole clear through you from bottom to top, you hear?"

Carrie crawled. When her head poked out into the wider tunnel, she almost yelped in surprise when she saw Shirley kneeling by the opening, finger on her lips. Regaining control, Carrie inched forward, tugging the man's left hand along with each jerk of her ankle.

Shirley flattened against the wall outside the hole, and as soon as the man's head appeared, she smashed a rock against it while Carrie rolled sideways. He made no sound at all as his head landed in the dust, and Shirley said, "I suspect he's only out for a moment, so where's that gun?"

"He's lying on it," Carrie said as they rolled him over. She started laughing. "His hand got stuck under him in the tunnel, he couldn't have shot me."

Shirley took the gun from the man's floppy hand, and he offered no resistance. "Okay, you got anything to tie him up with while I hold this gun?"

Carrie removed her shoelaces, then stuck her head back in the tunnel and called to Rob. When he arrived, they used the laces and strips of tape from the first aid kit in his backpack to secure their captive's hands and feet.

As soon as he was immobilized and the adrenaline rush of the moment was over, Shirley looked nervously around and said, "I'll go for help. Andy—the fella you said to find, Rob—has surely got here by now, and he's bringing an armed ranger with him. When I told him about what you saw behind that hole, he said the place would have to be guarded twenty-four hours a day until the area could be secured.

"So I said how to get here and came on ahead by myself while he put together what he needed. When I was still back a ways, that fella on the floor came walking along from the

other direction, and I hid to watch what he'd do. He noticed
the hole, looked through, then climbed in right away. That's
when I thought I'd best not wait for others to come, lest the
man mean trouble for you.

"I'd borrowed a flashlight from a pile of them in one
of the trucks back in the clearing. That was just because I
wanted to look through the hole and see what Rob found in
the cave room. But when this man went right in, I waited
a bit and climbed in after him. I heard you talking, so I
knew he'd heard you too. I came along, being as quiet as I
could manage and hiding my light with my fingers, trying
to memorize what I saw in his light up ahead. That part was
pretty bad since I couldn't see much, and I feel squished and
breathless in caves anyway.

"I guess Rob musta seen my light, because he sure
started talking loud. After that I didn't have to be so quiet.
When I got here I waited by the tunnel, wondering what
I should do next. I sure didn't want to crawl in that hole.
Then I heard the man say he had a gun and was bringing Carrie out. So I waited, and when he came through, I
whacked him."

Shirley looked around again. "You two gonna be okay
while I head back outside? All you gotta do is hold the gun
on him 'til someone comes to help." She handed Carrie the
gun and disappeared into the blackness.

Rob said, "I wasn't making up most of those reasons no
one wants to shoot a gun in here. A gunshot really could
cause more than one problem, and I didn't even think of
bullet ricochet." As the man started to wiggle, Rob continued. "So only shoot him if you have to. Hit him midsec-
tion."

Carrie said, "What you said back there sounded brilliant
to me. I had no idea guns could be so dangerous in caves."

"Well, I thought about Catherine and it made me feel
stronger. The ideas about a gun in the cave came after that."

"How did you know he wouldn't shoot us right off if
you talked back to him?"

"Didn't know for sure, but I had to do something, and
his tough talk sounded a lot like he'd heard it on TV." At
this their captive opened his mouth to swear. Rob said,
"Stop that! I don't want to hear from you, I can always shove
my dirty handkerchief down your throat." The man sub-
sided.

"I thought maybe he wasn't usually aggressive, wasn't
used to personal confrontation, and might be as scared and
nervous as I was." The man opened his mouth again, got out
a shouted, "Hey," before Rob pulled a disreputable piece of
wadded cloth from his pocket. The captive said no more.

"I'm really sorry, Mom. I knew nerves could make him
unstable, but things were so bad I had to try something. The
only way I could possibly overwhelm him would be with
talk."

"How did you know who he is and where he lives?"

"I didn't know for sure, but why would he have crawled
in this cave if he hadn't seen archeological treasure when he
looked in and wanted to profit from it? I couldn't think of
any other reason for him to come in here otherwise. I suspect his business is looting, and that house would be a prime
location for him. He probably has some cover though,
maybe another business or job."

"Do you suppose he had anything to do with Catherine's disappearance?"

"The action he took doesn't fit that, does it? I think he
was only interested in protecting what he saw in that cave
room for his own profit. If he's responsible for...for anything
to do with her or knows where she is, I don't think he'd be

hanging around this area right now."

They were silent for a couple of minutes, then Rob said, "Mom, will you be all right by yourself while I go back to work on that opening? The guy is tied securely. Stay close enough to him that, if he becomes a threat, you won't miss when you shoot."

The man said, "Hey, now," and Rob glared at him for a minute before continuing. "I saw something through the hole back there and maybe, well...it could be a person."

"You go ahead," Carrie said as her heart began pounding. *Catherine? Were they close?*

She was still feeling shaky from her encounter with the stranger, but thank goodness that didn't show in her voice. Rob disappeared through the tunnel, and in a minute she heard him chipping at plaster again.

Now Carrie was alone, with only the distant rumbling of the loader to keep her company. She wished she could lean against the cave wall, shut her eyes, and relax. Instead she blinked several times, focused her flashlight on the man, watched him breathe. She wanted to question him, but would talking be a good idea? He might distract her somehow, then break out of his bonds.

She wondered if he was the one who'd hit Rob on the head. He'd fallen into a sullen silence. Would he tell her anything if she asked him?

Time passed, and she began praying again. The cave was awfully quiet: she couldn't even hear the loader rumbling. What was Rob doing?

Finally she saw distant light in the tunnel. The noises of human movement grew louder, and she was glad Rob's chatter had been enough to cover Shirley's approach.

The two women who squeezed through the narrow passage into her part of the tunnel certainly surprised her, especially when she saw one of them was Shirley.

Answering Carrie's unasked question, Shirley said, "This is Patricia Selby. Andy was still churning out tons of words about his treasure and didn't want to leave it. We figured two people were needed to tote this fellow back to the opening. Pat, I mean Officer, uh, Ranger Selby gave her gun to Andy, radioed for help, and sort of deputized me to come back in here with her. But I promise you this is the last time."

After greeting Ranger Selby, Carrie said to Shirley, "Saying thank you isn't enough, but it's all I can think of at the moment."

"Shoot," was the only response. Then Shirley looked toward the small tunnel. "I guess Rob's gone on with the searching?"

Carrie nodded.

"Good," Shirley said. "Now you two get busy and find Catherine. Leave this ugly fella to us. He's not very big, and besides, it's possible we'll meet the emergency medical folks along the way. Andy is going to have a hissy fit when we drag him through his cave, though. Poor man, if it wasn't a matter of life and death..."

"Well, there's this," Carrie said, "if it weren't for these matters of life and death, we'd not have found the cave in the first place, and it might have been looted before he could find it himself."

Patricia Selby laughed as she replaced their captive's shoelace wrist ties with handcuffs and gave the laces to Carrie. "Oh, he understands that, but it doesn't make it any easier for him to accept contamination of an archeological site."

Carrie said nothing, and handed Selby the gun. The ranger checked it, stuck it in her belt, and then began unfolding a length of heavy plastic sheeting she'd been carrying. The three of them rolled the man onto it, and while Carrie watched, the other two women tugged him away along the tunnel, bumping over floor rocks without stopping.

As soon as they were gone, Carrie laced her shoes, then got down on her stomach and began crawling back toward the opening in the cave wall. When she reached the wider tunnel, the hole above the ledge was completely open, and Rob was nowhere in sight. She lifted the food tote, dropping it carefully near the now-silent doorway. Then, grabbing at rocks, she managed to pull herself up onto the ledge next to the tote.

She poked her flashlight through the opening and saw Rob, halfway around the wall, crouched over an almost unrecognizable form.

"Rob?" she said softly. "Is it...?"

He didn't look up. "She's here, Mom. We found her. She's breathing, but doesn't respond when I talk to her. Can you come to me very carefully? Don't disturb anything on the floor. She found...it's an infant burial room. Catherine must have discovered it before the cave-in."

He was silent for a moment before continuing. "Bring the water and tools with you. I'm going to need your help setting her free. I know now why she couldn't get out—some monster handcuffed her arm to a pipe." He bowed his head and said no more.

Chapter 24

CARRIE WORKED HER WAY carefully over floor bumps until she was beside Rob. She touched him on the shoulder and said, "Move aside and let me look at her. We don't know where she might be hurt."

"Her arm..."

"I see now. Horrible! What kind of person would..." Carrie stopped, overcome by emotion that closed her throat. After a minute she regained control, lifted her chin, and went on. "Can you release her without setting off a rock slide? It looks like she was protected from the cave-in by this little cubbyhole. Thank goodness for that much. She could have moved to safety in the cave room if it hadn't been for the handcuff. Brave, brave woman."

For a moment, neither of them said anything. Then Rob spoke, his voice low and rough. "I think I can at least break the handcuff away from the pipe. Hand me the geologist's pick." Using his left hand as a shield for Catherine's, he began hitting sharp blows against the chain.

While he worked, Carrie surveyed the cave room she'd just crossed. *Had Rob really said infants?*

She gasped. *Oh, dear Lord in heaven, those humps are all*

bundles with...dried babies in them. Rob was right.

Her mind, eager to hear Catherine's story and already full of unsatisfied riddles, now buzzed with more questions.

She heard a loud *chunk* from the pick, a ping, then silence. Rob said, "She's free." He beckoned when Carrie turned toward him. "Don't you think we can move her away from those rocks in the tunnel? She's got a blanket under her, so all we have to do is tug on the blanket."

She nodded and sat on the cave floor. Together they gently slid Catherine further into the niche. For a space of silence, unmarked by even the rumble of the loader, they studied the body lying between them.

Carrie broke the silence. "You've got the first aid kit over there. Why don't you clean off her wrist and bandage it? I'll wipe the dirt away from her face. I've got a cloth here, and water." She pulled Shirley's tablecloth and the water bottle out of the food sack, ripped off one end of the cloth, tore that in half, dampened a piece, then handed the second piece and the bottle to Rob.

Neither mentioned the fact that, except for a filthy jacket, Catherine was naked, her body covered only in layers of dirt. Her hair, looping wildly around her face, looked grey with collected dust.

Carrie wiped dirt away from Catherine's eyes, nose, and mouth, and when Rob handed the water bottle back to her, she began dripping water against her lips. "Catherine, Rob's here and you're safe. It's Carrie. Can you wake up now?" She kept talking softly as she alternately dripped water against Catherine's mouth and mopped up resulting rivulets running down her chin. After several minutes of this, she paused long enough to run her hands carefully over Catherine's body. "She's breathing evenly and nothing feels broken. I don't see any deep cuts except on her wrist. We

can't tell about her back, but I don't think we should turn
her over yet."

"The blood on her wrist was mostly dried," Rob said.
"I've cleaned the cuts and bandaged them as best I can. I
don't know if they need stitches. What should I do now? Go
for help? But we can't leave her."

Carrie, continuing to drop water against Catherine's
lips, reached into the food bag with her free hand and pulled
out the remaining piece of tablecloth. "How about covering her with this? And I don't see why we need to leave her.
Someone will come, or we can shout at the workers. They
surely must be getting close."

"I have clean clothes for her in my backpack," Rob said,
sounding almost cheerful. "Should I...?" He looked down.
"She's bruised and scratched all over, maybe it would hurt
her to put clothes on. I have panties and, well, I have a bra
too, and a shirt and jeans. What do you think? If strangers
are coming, she should be dressed in more than a tablecloth."

Carrie swallowed a giggle. Maybe it was only from tension, she didn't know, but Rob wouldn't understand giggles,
though, come to think of it, Catherine probably would.
"Let's wait before putting clothing on her until she wakes
up," she said, "unless you have socks. Her feet feel cold. And
if you have jeans we could fold them into a flat pillow for
under her head. I don't want to lift her head high enough to
put it in my lap until we're sure her back isn't injured."

"I have socks," Rob said, and he began digging in the
backpack while Carrie wiped Catherine's face with the damp
cloth again and went back to dripping water against her
lips. "I wish we had some lip balm," she said, "her lips are so
chapped."

"I have a tube of ChapStick in my pocket," Rob said.

"I'll fish for it as soon as I get these socks on...oh, MOM, her toes wiggled. I bet her feet are ticklish. Catherine, it's Rob, please come back to us. Wake up now. I'm sorry if I tickled your foot. I hate to be tickled, don't you? I won't do it again."

"Ummmm, Rob?"

It was a barely audible croak, but Catherine could have been shouting as far as Carrie was concerned. *Thank God. Oh, thank God!*

"Mom, did you hear that? She said my name! Hand me the water bottle and move over so I can sit closer to her face."

He replaced Carrie and began touching Catherine's face and hair, running the back of a finger along her cheeks and forehead, sliding a hand down her hair. "Hold your mouth still, love. I'm going to smooth some balm on your lips. Then do you think you can swallow a bit of water? Can you open your eyes? Are you hurting anywhere? I got your wrist free from that pipe, but I can't take the handcuff off yet. I know where there are keys though, I'll get them soon. You're safe now, you're all right. I'm here, and I promise I'll never go off and leave you again. I...oh, Mom, she blinked. Go ahead and open your eyes, Catherine. Can you see me? Do your eyes hurt? Oh, golly, I'll get this flashlight away from your face."

Catherine interrupted the torrent of words. "Drink," she said. Rob finally stopped talking, lifted the bottle, and began dripping water onto her tongue, giving her a minute to swallow between each two or three drops.

Carrie blinked her eyes and sniffled, glad for enough self-control to keep from sobbing. She'd never seen her son like this, wouldn't have said he was an especially tender man, but now he was pouring out tenderness as steadily as drips of water.

Guess he really has fallen in love with her, she thought. *Well, good.*

While Rob went back to babbling, Carrie looked more closely at the mine shaft as seen from her position just inside Catherine's niche. It looked like the collapse had stopped a few feet beyond them. The tunnel heading further into the hill appeared clear, and rough bracing timbers as large as railroad ties were visible over the top of the rock pile next to where she sat. Her flashlight beam stopped on a large metal tank lying on its side. One of the wooden support beams, almost buried in rocks, lay propped against it. Ah, then this had to be the source of the banging Rob heard. He was right, Catherine must have banged on the tank with a rock, attempting to summon help.

But then what happened here? What caused this part of the tunnel to collapse? Rob and Henry said they heard a sound like something metal falling just before the collapse. Was this tank standing upright until then? If so, why did it fall over?

Her flashlight surveyed the tank and illumined the pipe Catherine's wrist had been fastened to. Could Catherine have pulled the tank over? If so, why? Why would she...

A loud clang echoed along the tunnel. Carrie jumped, still thinking about the tank. Then she realized that the background noise of men's voices and the clang and rattle of rock removal now sounded very close. The loader started up, and this time the rumble and resulting vibration were frightening. The workers had made a lot of progress while her and Rob's attention was focused entirely on Catherine.

After several minutes, the rumbling of the loader faded away and the sound of wood being hammered replaced it. They must be building some kind of structure to shore up the ceiling.

"I hear the workers," she told Rob. "They're getting close. Thank goodness. That means we won't have to move Catherine back through all those convoluted tunnels or disturb any more of Dr. Fletcher's treasures."

Rob didn't look at her, but she knew he'd heard when he bent closer to Catherine's head and said, "Your rescuers are coming. Henry's helping them dig through the mine tunnel. I have fresh clothing for you in my backpack. I...do you mind if I wipe some of this dirt off and put on your underwear? I'll be very careful. All those men are coming here, and..."

Carrie heard what might have been an attempt at a laugh before the weak croak, "Clothes? Whatever...you think."

When Rob spoke again his voice was subdued and flat. "Catherine, did some man hurt you? Were you..."

Carrie saw Catherine struggle to raise her hand toward Rob's cheek and only make it as far as his arm. "Not raped, tell you later," she said, and closed her eyes.

Carrie moved her face next to the rock pile and shouted, "Henry, can you hear me?"

"Yes." He sounded startled. "Where are you?"

"Rob and I are not more than a few feet beyond you in the tunnel now. We got in another way and just found Catherine. She's been unconscious, but is waking up. We think she's okay for the most part."

Silence. The murmur of male voices, then Henry's shout.

"Carrie McCrite, do you mean that you've known another way in all along, that we did all this digging for nothing?"

Peeved? Oh, yes.

"Well, no, not for nothing. You still need to finish clearing. Catherine isn't ready to climb out the way we got in. And we came on a whim. I promise we didn't know...it was only by the grace of God that we reached her."

More male murmur. She could picture Henry giving a big sigh, maybe partly from relief.

"You say Catherine's okay?"

"Not exactly totally, but Henry, she will be soon, she will be."

"Good. If we keep working, will we send rocks down on you?"

"Nope, dig away; we're protected in a little niche, and a sort of cave room."

"All right, stand back."

"The mine looks open just beyond where we are, but I don't know how stable it is. We can move Catherine back a bit, but not much. We have some archeological treasures to preserve here. I don't know if the loader should come closer; I worry every time that thing rumbles. Seems like the whole area vibrates."

"Okay, we'll finish by hand. We have wheelbarrows, and most of the big stuff is moved outside now."

Another voice. "Mrs. McCrite, do you need medical help in there?"

"Well, I think she should have x-rays and be checked for injuries we can't see, plus get more liquid and nourishment in her. She has cuts that may need stitching. Otherwise she looks okay."

"We have an ambulance standing by. We found a man caught in the cave-in, and he's hurt pretty bad. Paramedics are with him now and he'll be going to the hospital too."

Behind her, Catherine moaned.

"Please hurry," Carrie shouted.

An answering "We hear you, and we'll be careful"

echoed along the tunnel before the sound of picks and shovels returned.

She crawled back to Catherine's side and noticed Rob
had been trying to ease panties over her legs. "Let me help
from the other side," she said. "If we work together to lift
her behind and then both of us pull, we won't twist her
body. But first, why don't you look for that chocolate bar in
the food tote and give her a nibble." She touched Catherine's
cheek. "Or would you rather have cheese?"

"Chocolate," Catherine murmured, and Carrie imagined
she saw her lips curve in a tiny smile.

Chapter 25

THEY GAVE UP ON the bra, but when Henry and the other workers broke through, Catherine had on underpants, a shirt, and socks. The remains of Shirley's tablecloth covered her from waist to knees.

At least she's covered, Carrie thought, *though for all I know the rest of us would be more embarrassed than Catherine herself if she were nude. Still, this is a chilly cave in Arkansas, not a French bathing beach.*

The men who—after much clamor—climbed over the remaining pile of debris to greet them didn't look at all like they were in a chilly cave. Dripping with sweat, dirty, and obviously exhausted though they were, they still appeared as triumphant heroes to Carrie. When Henry crawled through the opening for an awkward hug, she couldn't speak, and tears added to the sweat streaks on Henry's shirt.

It wasn't until after all the tumbling words and ideas settled into order and Catherine, quiet, but fully conscious, was being carried to daylight on a stretcher, that Carrie realized her son had disappeared.

It's over. She'll be all right. No matter how horrendous her expe-

riences, she'll be all right. She's so strong. And I'm...

The word *dirt* came to mind. Rob stopped walking and leaned against the bluff face, too weary to take another step. The urgent need to get away from everyone, especially his mother and Catherine, had moved him this far, but now...

Mom seems to think what I said to that guy back there in the cave was brilliant. It wasn't. It was dangerous and stupid. Catherine? I have no doubt she never wants to see me again, and I sure don't blame her for that. Why should I expect her to even like me after all that's happened? I really showed her my true colors, didn't I? How can I expect her to like me now? I can't like myself. And as for love...?

Rob rubbed his eyes with the backs of his hands. *When I think about what my selfishness did to her...and I haven't got the guts now to face hearing her story about...about being taken into that cave, chained to that pipe by some monster...*

Coward...coward. She must despise me.

Rob shook his head, thinking back to the hike when all this started. If only he could go back to the moment when he walked away from a wonderful, beautiful woman not far from this very spot.

Admit it Rob, you wanted to find something important, to be important!

He shook his head, kicked at a stone on the ground.

Worst of all, I may have shoved a man out of a bluffshelter to his death. Even if it was self-defense and he was an evil man, it was still killing a fellow human. I remember Henry saying he'd never be able to forget causing another's death, though finding and bringing down criminals was his job. He should know.

Rob heard shoes crunching on gravel and lifted his head to see a stocky man in a park uniform walking toward him. *What next?* He couldn't bear to meet anyone.

"Hello there," the newcomer said. "Are you one of the

workers who's helping dig through the cave-in? You look beat. Bad news?"

"I hear they made it through and found two people," Rob said, reluctant to admit who he was. "I guess the woman will be okay. They aren't sure about the man yet. Both are being taken to the hospital."

"Good, good." The ranger studied Rob's face as if trying to figure out what he saw there. His expression seemed wary, even a bit worried. After a pause he said, "It's been quite a day. We just arrested a man who was up to no good in one of our caves. A law enforcement ranger took him off in handcuffs—suspicion of looting archeological sites as well as threatening people with a gun. If charged, he'll be prosecuted under the Archeological Resources Protection Act. That's a federal law, you know. Could mean prison time."

The man's eyes stayed on Rob's face as he asked, "You new to this area? Visiting here?" and Rob realized the ranger might suspect he'd come upon another looter.

No reason I couldn't be one.

Rob sighed audibly, which heightened the man's interest in him.

"An older woman and one of our rangers brought the suspect out. They said he all but admitted he'd been looting sites here at the Buffalo."

Rob couldn't think of anything to say, and after an awkward silence the ranger took one hand off his walking stick and held it out. "My name's Andy Fletcher."

No! "Dr. Fletcher?" Rob was facing the man he least wanted to meet now and, for a wild moment, considered making up a name. Dr. Anderson Fletcher wasn't going to be pleased with any mediocre scientist who had caused untrained humans to compromise not one, but two, pristine archeological sites. It would definitely be best to give a fake name and slip away.

Coward, coward. Of course that won't work. We'll end up meeting sometime, somewhere, and I'll have dug myself into yet another deep hole.

"Rob McCrite," he murmured as he extended his hand. Maybe Fletcher wouldn't remember the name, for it had been some time since they spoke on the phone. Rob studied the archeologist. He was probably in his late forties; strong looking, square-jawed. No grey in the dark hair. While Rob watched, a grin lit Anderson Fletcher's face.

"Dr. Robert Amos McCrite? Hey, what good fortune. I'm glad to meet you. After you phoned last winter I looked you up on the 'net. Impressive. I read your dissertation, 'Cultural Ecology, Cultural Evolution, and Mobility in Prehistoric Peoples of the South-Central Plains.' Well done!"

He dropped Rob's hand and smiled. "Why don't you call me Andy, and say, did you get here at a good time! I have something exciting beyond words to share with you. Can you come with me back along the bluff? You know what they say: 'It's an ill wind that doesn't blow some good?' The concussion from the mine collapse proved that. It uncovered the opening to an overwhelming site that's probably been sealed away for at least three thousand years. I've barely looked at it thus far, I'm afraid of doing damage until I have the proper lighting and equipment, but I can already tell it will have an impact worldwide, especially in the archeological and anthropological communities. We'll be studying this site for years. It will provide an open window into at least one of the many ancient cultures that built their lives here along the Buffalo.

"I'm glad we ran into each other, Rob, since you, above all the people here, will understand the significance of what's been found, and know why I'm excited almost beyond speech." He laughed at the joke on himself and repeated, "*Almost* beyond speech," before he raced on. "I feel as if I've been given astonishing treasures, since research material and information we've had previously is quite spotty. Many sites here were cleaned out by early research teams or looted by individuals long before there was a National River. We have a big problem with looting now as well. We just don't have enough staff to protect 36,000 acres—you can imagine how it is—and the few looters that have been caught—well, most previous law enforcement didn't even amount to a slap on the wrist. Now it falls upon me to see that today's incredible find is protected. It's not going to be easy.

"Of course I need to make plans for professional study, and oh, the paperwork! People to notify, reports to file, compliance with the Native American Grave Protection and Repatriation Act." He shrugged. "Still, that's my job, and I'll gladly do it, especially if we ever find an intact burial site."

"You have no idea," Rob mumbled, then said aloud, "I understand." Reluctantly, not knowing what else to do, he stumbled after Andy Fletcher along the bluff base.

This man was here when Shirley and Ranger Selby came through his treasure room, so he knows some of its integrity has been breached. But he obviously doesn't know yet that I'm the one who breached it first, that I led the rest of them in. And when I tell him about the infant burial cave...

"Andy, is someone guarding the cave you spoke of now?"

"You bet. Armed ranger."

"Then can we stop here for a minute?"

"What is it? Hey, are you okay? I noticed you seem a little off-center."

Rob saw the man's look of concern and couldn't think what to say in return, so he just began to talk. "Let me tell you..."

"*Babies?* The woman who was saved from the cave-in...she found *babies?*"

"Yes, she uncovered the cave room while digging a niche in an attempt to save herself from the pending mine collapse. Seems like, in more than one place, those who dug the mine shaft broke into an existing cave system, and even when there was no breakthrough, the cave and mine tunnels are sometimes very close together, even side-by-side, as in the case of the infant burial room.

"I also believe some sites in the cave have already been found and looted, since it looked to me like the garage behind that house in the clearing was built to conceal an opening to the same system we're talking about. A Thunderbird parked in the garage earlier had a trunk full of ancient stone tools, some that appeared to be Dalton, as well as artifacts I guessed were Archaic. There was simple, unadorned pottery and even a few fiber pieces. I saw sandals, mats. But that car has disappeared now."

"My word," Andy Fletcher said, "I wonder if it's still in this area."

"Clyde Dunn radioed as much information as we had about the car to someone—sheriff, I think—before the mine clearing began, so they've probably found it by now. I'd bet that Thunderbird belongs to the man you just took into custody. If so, he must have concealed it near here. He probably has the keys in his pocket."

Andy nodded and said, "Good, good." Then he fell silent and stared at the ground for a few moments before saying, "I wonder what events or religious practices caused infants to be..."

Rob interrupted him, not interested in scientific musing at the moment. "I regret to say I've been in your treasure room and even broke down one large stone sealing it off

from the cave behind it. I had to get through, I was searching for my...for the woman caught in the cave-in, the one
who found the infant burial cave. Perhaps, in the overall
picture, there's no excuse for what I did, and I do regret
it. My mother was with me, and when we finally found
Catherine—the woman we were looking for—we had to
walk through the infant burial cave to get to her. Walked in,
very carefully, and not out. We waited there until they broke
through the rock piles and then were able to get out through
the main mine shaft."

"Oh." Now Fletcher looked straight into Rob's eyes.
"But to save a human life? That would always come first.
Besides, sounds like you being here had a lot to do with
finding the cave before looters cleaned it out."

The man's kindness made Rob feel worse. Well, at least
he had some compensating good news. "When I was going
through the tunnel behind that main storage room, I saw
three areas that looked as if they'd been sealed with the same
material we found in the main room you've already seen,
and at the infant burial site. I believe you have at least three
more locations that truly will be pristine when you break
through into them. Who knows what you'll find there."

For at least a minute, Andy Fletcher was speechless.

Rob continued. "I don't know if you've heard, but a few
days ago I was marooned in a shelter located near the top
of this bluff—back that way." He pointed. "While I was up
there, I began poking around a ceiling slab that had fallen,
and found what I thought was a Dalton scraper. There could
be more items under the slab. I'm sure looters have been
through the cave tunnels in that area, and they were definitely in the shelter. One of them hit me with a shovel and
knocked me out. But I don't believe they'd searched under
the slab yet."

"You have had a time of it...Dalton, you say?"

Rob hesitated, suddenly feeling uncertain. Had he been wrong? "Well, I'd had a blow on the head, was still fuzzy, but I think so. I left it there. Someone could rappel down and do a thorough search. And I'm positive there is a way to get to that bluffshelter from inside the cave system itself. When I was there, I heard sounds that indicate a connection.

"But what about jurisdiction? The bluffshelter is outside the National River boundary. I know the new opening to the storage room is on your land—I saw the boundary signs beyond it—but I guess you already knew that. Of course the clearing with the house and the cave entrance behind the garage are outside your boundary markers."

"It's obviously a huge cave system," Andy said thoughtfully. "We can tell where we are with GPS, but if anything of archeological significance is found in this area, the county sheriff would probably contact me anyway. I'm the only game in town, so to speak."

He laughed, and Rob found himself laughing too, which surprised him. Right now humor felt like icing over a dry and tasteless cake.

The laughter had concealed the sound of footsteps behind Rob. He jumped when Henry said, "Rob, shouldn't you be heading for the hospital now? Your mother went with Catherine in the ambulance and Shirley's following in her car. Shall we get your rental van and head that way too?"

Chapter 26

AFTER INTRODUCTIONS WERE made, Rob looked back at Henry for a moment, and Henry saw the eyes of a little boy who felt both guilt and fear. Or was he imagining that because he wanted to have a father's place in Rob's life? He did understand why Rob might feel guilt. Any human with a heart could, after what happened, but... fear?

The eyes also pleaded for something else Henry couldn't decipher, which left him off-balance and confused. What was Rob signaling? Had it come in response to the suggestion they head for the hospital to be with Catherine? Catherine? Something to do with Catherine now that she was safe? What...?

Catherine?

Rob knew that she probably wasn't seriously injured, so why would he be afraid for her?

Afraid? Afraid for... Afraid *of her*? But...

The moment passed as Rob turned to face Andy again. He held up both hands, palms out, and said, "I guess I'd better go along to the hospital. I'd like to view that room with you later, though. Maybe tomorrow?"

Andy Fletcher pulled a card from his wallet. "Here's my office phone. My cell won't work around here, but if you could phone me before nine in the morning I'll be doing paperwork in the office until at least then."

Rob pocketed the card, said, "Okay, thanks," and formal manners suddenly replaced scientific interests. They shook hands all around, everyone made polite comments about how glad they were to meet, and then Rob and Henry headed off toward the parking lot where they'd left the rental van.

Neither of them spoke for some time. By now Henry felt like—if not a stepfather—at least a very good friend to Rob, and he was hoping there would be a way to help him through this obviously rough patch. He'd always been sensitive to others' moods, so during the silence he tried to sort out a reason for Rob's distress.

His ability to read other people had been a big help in police work, and also in life with Carrie. With his first wife, Irena the Icy, he hadn't cared enough to pay attention. Now Rob certainly had all his attention. Henry was conscious of underlying distress, but not yet sure of the reason for it. Finally he said, "They think Catherine will be okay once she has enough liquid, food, and rest."

"Yes."

"The cuts and bruises will heal, but...there could be lingering trauma, even nightmares. I saw some of that in police work."

"Oh." Rob turned to look at him. "I didn't think about that." Now his eyes went puppy-dog sad. After a long silence, he asked, "When is Shirley going home?"

"Tomorrow morning."

"Are you moving in with Mom then?"

"I thought I might. Unnecessary for her to be there

alone."

"Yes."

Henry paused, feeling his way. "The cabin sleeps six, or if you use the couch, seven."

"I see."

More silence.

Henry asked, "When is Catherine due back in her office?"

"Not until next Monday."

"Well then, if she doesn't need to be in the hospital long, she can move to the cabin too. Don't you think it would be best for her, under the circumstances? Carrie will probably suggest it. The two of them can spend quiet time together while I fish and you explore with Dr. Fletcher."

Rob said nothing.

"So, we'll wait and see what Catherine wants to do, okay?"

"Yes."

Henry went on cautiously. "If you like, you could move to the cabin too. It doesn't have private rooms, but there are three double beds, two upstairs and one down, so I suppose it's as private as a camp ground. And, if there were nightmares, we'd all be there to..."

Rob interrupted him with a blown-out puff of air.

After that, they hiked in silence until they reached the van. As soon as they were moving, Rob said, "I'd like a shower and shave before we go on to the hospital, so I'm heading for Tyler Bend first. I feel like *dirt*."

Henry was aware of a possible double meaning in Rob's emphasis on the word *dirt*, but he didn't acknowledge it. "We'll both take time to clean up," he said. "The girls can easily handle the hospital stuff until we get there. I'll call Carrie as soon as we're out of this valley and tell her our plans. If she's with Catherine, she can explain to her why you haven't arrived yet. Then, while we're at Tyler Bend, I'll take time to stop at the visitor center and thank Shane."

"Who?"

"Ranger Shane Lind, you've seen him there. He's the man who kept me from falling apart when the two of you first went missing. I suppose he knows Catherine has been found, but if not, I can bring him up to date."

"Oh. Probably I should thank him too. And I want to buy one of their flower identification books for Catherine."

"Good idea. Better than taking her flowers."

"Uhh, I didn't think about flowers. Should I send her some? I..."

"Send flowers? Seems to me she'd much rather have you there, handing her the book. Besides, she'll be so glad to see you she won't care about gifts."

After a long silence Rob said, "She won't be glad to see me, and she shouldn't be."

"*Shouldn't be?* What do you mean? Why not?"

"Your memory isn't that short, Henry. I'm the one who left her to suffer everything that's happened, and I don't suppose we've heard the half of it yet."

"Y'know," Henry said, speaking slowly but thinking as fast as he could, "it's my observation that the women in our lives...our women...have a lot of forgiveness built into them. My daughter Susan, your mom, and Catherine. They put stuff behind them and move on. Catherine has never once mentioned my thirty-plus years spent ignoring her existence."

"No?"

"No."

Silence again. Henry wondered if Catherine really did forgive him. Neither of them had ever discussed those missing years.

"Huh, none of *our women* as you put it—and we both know Mom and Catherine would hate being referred to like that—have been put into life-threatening danger through neglect from one of us until now. Catherine has experienced that this week, and all of it caused by me, the man sitting next to you. That is very different from anything else, Henry. Call me a coward...okay, I am. I haven't the courage right now to face Catherine, knowing what I've done. I can't bear to see how she'll look at me."

"Oh, come on, Rob, the man or men responsible for what happened to her are the ones who dragged her into that mine, put the handcuffs on her, ripped her clothes off."

"But if I'd been there... People who hike in back country are advised not to hike alone. I know that, but I didn't pay any attention. Trust me, Catherine King is smart enough not to need Rob McCrite in her life. If I do go to see her, she'll either be icy polite or tell me what I caused in minute detail."

"You think? Well, I don't. Besides if she does give you a bad time—and I'm sure she won't—maybe that's a way of getting it out of her system and over with. So, you should try her out and see. Give her a chance."

"Sorry, no, I can't do it."

Henry's first impulse was to affirm Rob's own statement that he was a coward, but he said nothing, and took out his cell phone to call Carrie.

"Oh, gee, Henry, I'm glad you called, and it's fine from this end if you want to stop over at Tyler Bend. We're doing very well. A doctor is checking Catherine now, and I hope someone is cleaning her up. The report's good so far. In fact, after they work on replacing lost fluids and watch her overnight, they say she can come back to the cabin with me.

Right now Shirley and I are entertaining a law enforcement ranger and two sheriff's deputies who're waiting to talk with her as soon as she's settled in a room."

"That's good news, my little love. When we finish at Tyler Bend we'll take the rented truck back, then walk to the hospital. See you soon."

After Henry reported this conversation to Rob, the two men spent the rest of the drive to Tyler Bend lost in their separate, private thoughts.

Not long after Rob and Henry left the truck rental agency, Rob's steps slowed. He seemed to be mulling something over, so Henry didn't disturb him until they reached the hospital's entrance area.

"What next?" Henry asked.

Rob shrugged. "I'll stop at the office and check myself out, sign whatever papers they require, get my wallet back. You go ahead. Find Mom and Shirley and see what's going on with Catherine.

"Here, hand her the wildflower book for me, tell her I'm glad she's safe now. When I've finished checking out, I'll get supper in the cafeteria and then wait here in the lobby for you. Unless you want to eat with me?"

"No, not yet. We finished all the lunch leftovers before I came to find you back at Rush. I think I'll wait and eat later with Carrie and Shirley. Maybe you'd like to get dessert with us then."

Henry cleared his throat and continued, "When the law enforcement folks have heard all they want from Catherine and the rest of us upstairs, I'm sure they'll want to talk with you. I'll tell them where you are if you still think you don't want to come up...?"

"No. I'll be here."

After one look at Rob's miserable face, Henry managed
only a nod. He wished he could talk with Carrie right now.
Maybe she'd think of something to say that would wake her
son up. All that came into his head at the moment was an
urge to either swat Rob on the behind or hug him and say
something comforting.

But neither of those would be right, he was smart
enough to know that. Doing nothing was safer right now.
Maybe it meant he was a coward, too.

Henry took the wildflower book, gave Rob a light
squeeze on the arm, and turned toward the information
kiosk.

Chapter 27

"WHERE'S ROB?" Carrie was in the hall getting a drink of water when Henry left the elevator, and, after Henry answered her question, astonishment took over.

"He said *what?* Are you sure?"

She stared at him as he repeated, "Rob says he's not coming up to see Catherine. He's convinced she won't want anything to do with him after what happened. Since he blames himself for all this mess, he thinks she must too."

Carrie's first impulse was to rush to the main lobby, yank Rob up, and drag him to Catherine's room. But of course that wouldn't be a good idea at all, even assuming it worked. "Dear God. If he'd just talk with her like I have. Why won't he...? Well, what can I do? Maybe if I talked to him, told him...?"

Henry frowned. "You can kind of understand why he feels the way he does. He knows people hiking off a regularly used trail should travel in pairs, but, in his focused enthusiasm, he left her behind anyway. I hate to say this, especially to you, but in a large sense, it is his fault. If they'd been together the entire time, none of this bad stuff would have happened to either of them."

Carrie's shoulders slumped and she murmured, "I know, I know. But I'm his *mother*. I need to do something, make him see...get him to talk with her, hear her side."

Henry continued, "I don't think it's a good idea to force the issue right now. And I didn't say anything to him about agreeing the blame is partly his. Instead I pointed out that the man...was it just one man?"

"Yes. Catherine calls him 'The Monster.'"

"It fits. Anyway, I told him the man who abducted her, cut her clothes off, and handcuffed her to the pipe in the mine was the one at fault. And that's true, after the fact."

"Henry, I've had such hope for those two. I feel perfectly awful, partly, I guess, because I don't know the best thing to do to fix this. It's complicated and touchy, isn't it? Saying one wrong word could make everything worse than it is. *What can I...what can we do?*"

He was silent for a moment before answering. "My love, I think Rob has to do this himself—he has to figure it out. For an adult male, well, you are aware your son hasn't had much practice facing the world or the female of our species outside academia? He's so career-focused. I'm sure the University loves him for that, but it makes for one heck of a social life and messes up meaningful personal relationships. It even caused some of our problems here." He cleared his throat. "This experience with Catherine is new territory for him, isn't it?"

Carrie knew the experience Henry meant didn't refer to the terrible events of the past few days, and she nodded. "We talked about that very thing when I visited him in the hospital here yesterday. I apologized then for not encouraging him to take part in more social activities when he was in high school. You know what he told me? He said it wouldn't have mattered because he usually wasn't invited anyway."

She stared at the floor. "Now I want to weep for that boy from the past. He's paying today for what he missed then. We both are. And, Catherine is too, of course.

"Henry, come sit with me here in the waiting area while I think about what can be done."

They chose a leatherette couch in the empty seating area, and Carrie bowed her head. After a few moments of silence, Henry reached for her hand.

"Cara, I think this isn't a time when you're supposed to take any overt action."

She jerked her head up and stared at him. "Overt! Henry King, you are an answer to prayer. Overt action, no. But I was just thinking yesterday that mothering can be covert activity, especially when kids are grown."

He laughed. "Okay. Covert. Couldn't prayer be in that category?"

"Ummm, maybe so." She was silent again as she began the mental climb from what had seemed like a pit of help-lessness. Henry was right, of course. After another minute she said, "All right, except for covert activity, I'll leave it to the two of them. I promise you, I really will."

He bent to kiss her on the forehead, and she managed a smile. "Now then, I need to bring you up to date on what's been going on since we got to the hospital."

"Yes, please do."

"First, and most important of all, Catherine does love Rob, or at least she sure thinks she does. And you know why she brought that ceiling down? It was to save his life and yours. But I guess I shouldn't tell him that, he'll just feel worse."

"How did she...?"

"I'll get to it in a minute. The man who took her in the mine warned that the boiler was bracing part of the ceiling,

and moving it would cause a collapse. After he'd been gone
a long time, and banging on the boiler hadn't brought any
response, she figured out that she could dig a safety niche to
shelter in and then pull the boiler over. She thought the falling boiler, together with the impact of the collapsing ceiling
beam and rocks, might break loose the pipe she was handcuffed to. If it did, then she could climb out over the debris
pile. But that was before the man called Al came into the
mine and found her. He was talking to her when they both
heard Rob shouting. Al pulled out a gun and started back
toward the mouth of the cave where you two were. To stop
him she pulled the tank over right then."

Henry simply shook his head and said nothing.

"She says Al planned to kill her so he didn't mind talking. He was a partner in a large looting operation—three
men at least. The man who forced her into the mine and
planned to assault her sexually was another partner. Al indicated that her captor had become a threat to their operation
because of his womanizing. Catherine's sure Al is the one
who killed the man, although he never admitted it in so
many words.

"Catherine identified a photo of the body at the foot of
the bluff as the man who kidnapped her. The sheriff's deputy
told us he was stabbed with his own knife before someone
pushed him off the edge. The blade hit him in the heart.
Rob's backpack fell with him, and the missing watch and
cell phone were inside. I think that means the man who hit
Rob was also Catherine's captor, and he'd stolen Rob's watch
and cell phone before he was killed. Therefore Rob was
already unconscious when Al came into the shelter through
the cave system. Rob couldn't have caused the fallen man's
death."

Henry drew in breath and whooshed it out. "Am I

glad. As a law officer I've been down that road, and it's not something I'd wish on anyone. By the way, I wasn't able to ask Shane about the dead man this afternoon because Rob was with me the entire time I was in the Tyler Bend Visitor Center. I'm glad you found out what happened."

"Henry, the man who came in the cave just before Rob found Catherine, the one Shirley bopped on the head, has to be in the same group of looters. The house and garage in that clearing are his, after all. No one has said anything to us about him yet, but he has to be part of it."

"Yes, I'm sure you're right. Now then, Cara, don't you think we have to tell Catherine what Rob's state of mind is right now? Why he's not coming to see her?"

"Oh, golly, I don't know." She sighed. "But then, we will have to explain it eventually, won't we?"

"Of course we will. At least if he persists in his refusal to 'face the music,' you might say. But tell me, how is she doing, really?"

"Amazing. Except for bruises and scratches and the cuts on the top of her wrist, she seems bright as a new penny. Evidently rationing her water wisely helped stave off major dehydration, and they've been giving her fluids and nourishment through those tube things, though they told us that's only short term. She says she's ready to come back to the cabin with me as soon as they let her leave the hospital. She doesn't want to return to her tent, so Rob's on his own there."

"I've already told him Catherine would probably stay with us after Shirley went home."

"*Us?* Oh, Henry, I'm so glad you're coming to the cabin. I didn't realize how much I'd miss my big Huggy Bear." She hesitated. "Our house sure felt empty without you, so I guess I've gotten used to having you around."

He laughed and squeezed her hand. "I suggested to Rob that he move in with us too. I told him Catherine might have problems with nightmares; I've seen that in others who endured great stress. I hinted he might be able to help her. You know, with a bit of judicious cuddling?"

"Oh, my! Well, I guess I *can* see how, if she does have nightmares—and I'm inclined to think she won't—it would be nice to have someone close by to hold her and tell her everything is okay. Not that I couldn't do that, of course."

"Still..."

"Hmmm, yes." She changed the subject. "Honestly now, do you think they have any suspicion Rob might have killed that man? After all Al hasn't confessed and may never do so. A deputy is staying with him in case he regains consciousness and can say anything."

"From what you have said, any fatal action by Rob seems impossible."

"But, thinking like they might, well, do they suspect my boy could have stabbed him?"

"Carrie, come on...Rob says he was hit on the head as soon as he reached the shelter, and no one has any reason to doubt that. I can see him shoving someone over the edge almost in a reflex action, but to stab a man through the ribs and reach his heart? Hunh-unh. Not possible. That takes skill, force, and directed aim. Rob simply couldn't do it. Besides, the watch and cell phone prove he didn't."

"So that worry is over, thank goodness. We need to let him know."

"Exactly." He stood up. "Let's go to Catherine's room first. I want to see her."

"Are we going to tell her about Rob?"

"Don't you think we have to?"

"Well, yes."

"Then which one of us...?

"You do it, Henry. You're the one who talked with him."

He sighed. "I expected you to say that. But you can't find fault with how I put it."

"I promise you—I won't."

Chapter 28

CATHERINE'S ROOM SEEMED full of women. Shirley sat by the bed holding Catherine's uninjured hand, National River law enforcement was represented by Ranger Patricia Selby, and one of the sheriff's deputies was female. The lone male deputy stood against the wall taking notes.

Carrie's age meant she instantly saw this as a reversal of role stereotypes she'd endured all her life, and she wanted to pump her arm in the air and shout, "*Yes.*"

But of course she didn't.

Patricia Selby said, "Oh, good, we've just finished talking with Ms. King and are eager to hear about your part in this now." She stretched to look around Henry. "Will Rob McCrite be along soon? We need to talk with him, too."

Henry glanced at Catherine and said, "He's checking himself out of the hospital. He left here rather abruptly yesterday afternoon without going through the normal formalities. You'll find him waiting for you down in the main lobby."

Henry's eyes caught Catherine's puzzled look, but she said nothing.

Selby introduced the two deputies, and then went on. "Mr. King, will you tell the three of us your part in all this? We know your concern began when Rob McCrite and Catherine King didn't return for a planned supper with you at Tyler Bend. We know what you were doing after that, up to the time Rob McCrite was found in the bluffshelter, but can you tell us about events beginning when the hospital phoned you to say he was missing?"

"In a minute." Henry went to Catherine's side and said, "Hello, baby sister. Nice to see you in the daylight." He stopped there, not knowing what more to say.

"Hiya." She grinned. "Go ahead and talk to these guys. Hearing everyone tell their part of the adventure catches me up with what went on while I was stuck in that wretched mine."

Shirley released Catherine's hand and got up. "Carrie and I have been making over her long enough, it's your turn now. Have a seat."

So he did, and began talking about Rob's arrival at Tyler Bend, about Al at the camp site, about the silver Thunderbird and truck, about their trip to Rush, Rob's agitation, and his conviction that he knew how to locate Catherine. He told about finding the cave opening, hearing noises, the mine cave-in. "Then the workers came to clear the mine, and you know all about that."

"So," Patricia Selby said, turning to Carrie. "Ms. Booth has told us about what happened after you three went to check the new opening in the bluff face, but she wasn't with you the whole time. Would you describe all that went on inside the cave before I got there?"

Carrie repeated every detail she could remember. She watched Henry's frown deepen while she told about the man with the gun, though a smile broke through after she got to the part where Shirley clobbered him on the head.

Everyone was quiet while she described the finding of
Catherine, and her voice stuttered with emotion when she
tried to convey her feelings, and what she had observed in
her son. At some point during the telling, Henry reached for
Catherine's hand.

When Carrie finished, Selby said, "Well, we only need
to hear from one more person to finish the story, and that's
Rob McCrite. You say he's down in the lobby?"

"Yes." Henry looked his wife and sighed. It had to be
said. He then faced Catherine while he answered Selby.

"Right now he feels overwhelmed by guilt because his
actions—hiking away from Catherine—caused untold ago-
ny for her, not to mention problems for himself and lots of
other people. Criminals were stopped, of course, but he's fo-
cusing more on the rest of the story. We have one dead man,
another severely injured, the need for an elaborate mine
clearing operation, and the involvement of law enforcement
throughout a couple of counties, all largely because of his
one simple action—so yes, he's more or less hiding out in
the lobby. Do you blame him?"

No one said anything for at least sixty seconds. He
glanced from Carrie to Catherine. Carrie bobbed her head
at him, and he decided it must be a nod of encouragement.
Catherine looked thoughtful and chewed the inside of her
lip.

Then Shirley spoke up. "Hmmm, carrying a bucket
load of poop, isn't he? But who can say, in this life, what
one thing really leads to another and what causes what?
Something had to stop those looting guys and the oversexed
demon. Besides, look what we gained...just ask Dr. Fletcher
about that. As for this woman in the bed here, well, she
doesn't look permanently damaged to me.

"So you three, go on and leave now. You head down to the lobby to question Rob McCrite all you want. I think we need us a little family conference here."

"Yes, we do," Catherine said, "and family includes you, Shirley Booth. If Rob's going to sit down there in sackcloth and ashes, well, then, I have a few ideas..."

Before Patricia Selby reached the door, Shirley added one more sentence. "Don't you say anything to that young man about guilt or our family conference, you hear?"

After nods all around, the ranger and deputies disappeared down the hall.

Rob was pretending to read a magazine when Shirley, Carrie, and Henry walked into the lobby.

"You eat?" Henry asked.

"Yes, pretty good salmon cakes," Rob said.

"We decided to go to Neighbor's Mill for supper. You might as well wait for us here. Their food is already prepared, so we won't be long. By the way, that guy who fell out of the bluffshelter was stabbed first. They know you had nothing to do with his death."

Rob said, "The deputy told me. Thanks." Before he could continue Carrie said, "Catherine's sound asleep now. They took the tubes out and probably gave her a pill so she'll sleep through the night. We'll peek in on her when we get back, then all of us can head for Tyler Bend and our beds."

Rob had started to stand, thinking he might ride along with them to the Mill, but they were out the door before he was fully on his feet. "Hmpf," he said and dropped back into his chair, dangling the magazine in one hand.

For a couple of minutes he sat quietly. Then he laid the magazine aside and walked toward the information kiosk.

One step inside the room. Two steps. Her hair was spread over the pillow, a cascade of dark waves. He thought of Autumn Moon.

A third step. She was breathing evenly. A bruise on her cheek, bandage on her forehead, otherwise...

A fourth step and he looked straight down at her. So beautiful...

Two brown eyes opened. One winked. "Hiya," she said.

"Oh." He jerked back as if she'd poked him with a cattle prod.

"Oh, indeed. So you finally came to face me, the wronged woman."

Rob winced. "Oh, dear God. I can't..."

"Can't what?"

"Can't..." He backed up one step.

"Here now, don't leave. Help me sit up. You push that button on the bed." She pointed.

"I..."

"It isn't hard, Rob, even for a college professor. Push the button. Please?"

"I..." He couldn't seem to get anything more out.

"You said that. See there, pushing the button wasn't hard, was it? Now if you lean over here and put your arms under mine, you can help me shift up in the bed. My underpants are slippery against the sheet, and things are a little sore, here and there. So, if you put your arms around me..."

Speechless, he did as she asked, and she leaned into him, all softness supported by his arms, sliding back against the pillows until she was sitting erect.

"Good. Now, won't you have a seat?" She indicated the chair Henry had vacated a few minutes earlier.

"Catherine, I shouldn't be here, I'm just a bad memory, I'm sorry..."

"Mmm. I guess you did have a rough time in that bluff-shelter, getting hit on the head, losing your watch and cell phone. But it turned out to be like you described to me on the walk to the Indian Rockhouse, didn't it? You found good stuff?"

He was too astonished to say a thing.

"I found good stuff too," she said in a matter-of-fact tone. "I gather Dr. Anderson Fletcher is more than pleased with us and what we discovered.

"And, of course we should be pleased with us too."

"You're *pleased?*"

"Rob, your conversational skills seem to have dropped out of sight while you were up in that bluffshelter. Yes, pleased. Aren't you? Think of what we accomplished."

She was silent for a moment, staring at the top of his bowed head. When she spoke again, her voice was soft. "Rob, we won, *we won!* Yes, it was awful in that mine, yes, there were times when I was discouraged, sick to death, terrified, even a little out of my head. I'm sure you know exactly what I mean."

Now he looked up at her, nodded, and said, "After I learned you were missing it was like I'd dropped into hell."

She smiled. "I'm grateful you care that much, Rob McCrite. I'm grateful we both do. But coming out of it as victors is what matters. I feel like, well, like queen of the Amazons right now. The world threw its worst at me and I beat it. Don't you feel that way, too? I hope you understand, because no one else, not your mom, or Henry, or Shirley, can share this with us. I wouldn't even try to explain it to them. *We faced evil and we beat it!*"

"Catherine..."

The next thing he knew he was sitting on the bed and they were hugging and crying, and he was saying, over and over, "Autumn Moon, my Autumn Moon."

But by the time Carrie, Henry, and Shirley walked into the room, Rob was sitting sedately in the visitor chair, and the two of them were busy speculating about the significance of some of the treasures they had seen in the cave.

Only the funny, knowing whispers of smiles on their faces gave anything away, and Carrie, Henry, and Shirley were far too wise to comment about that.

The End

The Truth Behind the Truth: Epilogue

Caven Clark, Ph.D.
Archeologist/Curator
Buffalo National River

ARCHEOLOGY IN A NATIONAL PARK unit pro-
vides the backdrop to Ms. Nehring's tale, *A River to Die
For.* The looting of sites and of caves and bluffshelters in
particular is a very real problem at Buffalo National River,
beginning well before it became part of the NPS in 1972
and continuing to the present, and alas, into tomorrow.
There was a time, not so long ago, when digging and collection of prehistoric and historic archeological sites was not
wrong and was not illegal. It was part of the local culture
and often was undertaken during a family outing on Sun-
days after church. It was just something that people did
when surrounded by the richness of a prehistoric material
culture equaled only by the arid regions of the American
Southwest and Great Basin. Stories of coffee cans full of
arrowheads abound, and many a collection still graces the

mantle of an old home, or a wall in a local restaurant. I find no fault with these people.

But times have changed. "Collectors" are now "looters," and instead of a family pastime the activity has become the domain of persons also dedicated to drug production and distribution, poaching, and other criminal activities. My job as an archeologist is no longer the digging of square holes for the extraction of scientific data, but the struggle to leave as much in the ground as is possible: in other words, to preserve what remains of the past for future generations. This is not preservation for future generations of looters, but for a public that includes both park visitors interested in the Buffalo River's past as well as a scientific public that responsibly recovers and interprets these remains.

Most park visitors don't arrive with Rob's foreknowledge of local archeological sites, nor with his massive sense of responsibility (and guilt) towards their protection. You won't find burial caves with infants anywhere along the Buffalo. But the rest of the account is contextually accurate. I am grateful to Ms. Nehring for the opportunity to provide professional input for this story, for an opportunity to "get the message out" that preservation is the key, and stewardship is the vehicle for protecting these sites in perpetuity.

Carrie's Recipes

CARRIE'S BAGGIE OMELETS

For each omelet you'll need:

> 1 one-quart zip lock freezer bag
> 2 eggs
> Whatever you like in an omelet: chunks of onion, green
>   pepper, bacon, black olives, etc.
> Shredded cheese of choice
> Salt and pepper
> And...one large kettle of already boiling water. (Rolling
>   boil.)

If you are using onions, sauté lightly or soften in the microwave. Cook any meat you have selected. Chop everything you are adding to your omelet into small pieces.

Break two eggs into a baggie. Seal, removing as much air as possible. Squeeze and squish until eggs are well mixed.

Open baggie and add vegetables, meats, and seasonings you have selected.

Seal bag again, removing air, and squish to mix.

Drop bag(s) in kettle of boiling water and boil for exactly thirteen minutes. Remove from water and roll omelet out on a plate. If you wish, add shredded cheese immediately.

CARRIE'S HOLIDAY SALAD

One can jellied cranberry sauce
2 packages raspberry gelatin (or one double package)
1 bag frozen raspberries, thawed, with whatever juice
    they make
One-half cup raspberry yogurt (if not available, use
    plain)

Dissolve gelatin in three cups hot water. Using wire whisk, stir in the can of jellied cranberry sauce, cutting and stirring until it's mostly blended into the hot gelatin. Add yogurt and blend. Stir in thawed berries and juice. (Juice should not exceed one-half cup.) Pour into an attractive serving bowl and chill, stirring occasionally to be sure berries stay blended throughout the gelatin.

(If you like a sweeter salad, sprinkle sugar on berries as they thaw, but be sure the sugar is dissolved before you stir berries into the gelatin mixture.)

About the Author

AWARD-WINNING ARKANSAS writer and journalist Radine Trees Nehring and her husband, photographer John Nehring, live in the rural Arkansas Ozarks near Gravette.

Nehring's writing awards include the Governor's Award for Best Writing about the State of Arkansas, Tulsa Nightwriter of the Year Award, and the Dan Saults Award, which is given by the Ozarks Writers League for nature- or Ozarks-value writing. The American Christian Writers named Nehring Christian Writer of the Year in 1998, and Oklahoma Writers Federation, Inc., named her book *Dear Earth* Best Non-Fiction Book. Her novels, *A Valley to Die For* and *A Wedding to Die For* both earned Best Mystery Novel awards from OWFI. *A Wedding to Die For* was also nominated by Deadly Ink for a David G. Sasher award for Best Mystery Novel, 2006. *A Valley to Die For* was a 2003 Macavity Award nominee for Best First Novel.

Research for her many magazine and newspaper features and her weekly radio program, *Arkansas Corner Community News*, has taken the Nehrings throughout the state. For more than twenty years Nehring has written non-fiction about unique people, places, and events in Arkansas. Now, in her Something To Die For Mystery series, she adds appealing characters fighting for something they believe in and, it turns out, for their very lives.

Radine Trees Nehring is a member of Ozarks Writers League, Sisters in Crime, Authors Guild, and represents the state of Arkansas on the Board of Mystery Writers of America, Southwest Chapter.

OTHER BOOKS BY ST KITTS PRESS

A WEDDING TO DIE FOR BY RADINE TREES NEHRING

Carrie and Henry's wedding at the Crescent Hotel in Eureka Springs, Arkansas, is threatened by a bombing, a murder, and a ghost bride wearing red.

THE OKLAHOMAN (REVIEWED BY KAY DYER) "...a lively, suspenseful few days at a top Arkansas tourist spot."

OZARKS MAGAZINE (REVIEWED BY LEE KIRK) "If you have already made the acquaintance of Carrie McCrite and Henry King, you won't want to miss their wedding. If you're not familiar with Radine Trees Nehring's senior citizen sleuths, you're in for a very good read."

THE OZARKS MOUNTAINEER (REVIEWED BY JIM VERITAS) "With writers like [Nehring], the Ozarks doesn't need to hire advertising agencies to promote the area."

MIDWEST BOOK REVIEW (REVIEWED BY SHELLEY GLODOWSKI) "... a mystery that is cozy and fascinating at the same time... Nehring has produced another winner!"

THE GRAVETTE NEWS HERALD (REVIEWED BY GAYLE WILLIAMS) "...*A Wedding to Die For* starts off with a bang. The action and interest doesn't slow down until the last page. Actually, not even then!"

PASSPORT JOURNAL (REVIEWED BY CROW JOHNSON EVANS)
"Thought-provoking, entertaining, chilling, and steamy—Radine Trees Nehring's book redefines the cozy mystery and upends misconceptions about age, murder, foreigners, northwest Arkansas, community and romance."

I LOVE A MYSTERY (REVIEWED BY EDEN EMBLER) "The author manages to teach by the depiction of the kind of characters who are honorable, caring and worth knowing, without in any way being preachy...HIGHLY RECOMMENDED."

MYSTERY LOVERS CORNER (REVIEWED BY DAWN DOWDLE)
"...great senior sleuths...I can't wait to read more in this series."

MYSTERIES GALORE.COM (REVIEWED BY NANCY EATON)
"...filled with suspense and loaded with fun."

CAROLYN HART (AUTHOR OF THE DEATH ON DEMAND AND HENRIE O MYSTERIES) "Readers will delight in Carrie McCrite, a spunky heroine who faces danger and finds love. A pleasure awaits mystery lovers."

PATRICIA SPRINKLE (AUTHOR OF THE THOROUGHLY SOUTHERN MYSTERIES) "Nehring's delightful novel features history and romance with murder thrown in. A winning combination and fun read."

JOE DAVID RICE (ARKANSAS TOURISM DIRECTOR) "Radine Trees Nehring's superb mysteries really capture the pulse of the areas they're set in."

DORIS ANN NORRIS (LIBRARY LIAISON FOR SISTERS IN CRIME)
"A very pleasant read and wonderful characters. If you

haven't read this series, do so. I also love the Arkansas settings of the novels. It makes me want to go there..."

A Treasure to Die For by Radine Trees Nehring

An Elderhostel at Hot Springs, Arkansas, is turned upside down when Carrie disappears in steaming water and Henry goes hunting.

Library Journal "Lovers of cozy mysteries with colorful characters will want this third title in Nehring's 'Something to Die For' series (after *A Valley To Die For, Music To Die For*)." (reviewed by Tamara Butler)

The Ozarks Mountaineer "The mystery is as hot as Hot Springs' springs, and the characters are as natural and well-drawn as a hot bath in one of the town's historic bathhouses." (reviewed by Jim Veritas)

Midwest Book Review "Nehring puts together a very entertaining whodunit in *A Treasure to Die For*...A good read." (reviewed by Shelley Glodowski)

Ozarks Magazine "...a fun read."

I Love a Mystery "I enjoy seeing older protagonists, and the author makes the area so intriguing I want to go see it for myself. RECOMMENDED." (reviewed by Eden Embler)

The Pilot "...features 'regular' people...The characters are likeable...the books tell an interesting story as well as offering well-researched historical background...Nehring has hit on a good combination." (reviewed by Faye Dasen)

Gravette News Herald "If you haven't read Radine's first two books in the series, you're missing a lot. Get to know Carrie and Henry and don't miss this third book." (REVIEWED BY GAYLE WILLIAMS)

THE BENTON COUNTY DAILY RECORD "Along with good, tight story-telling, the writer highlights some of the most interesting locations in Arkansas where her stories take place." (REVIEWED BY TONYA McKIEVER)

PATRICIA SPRINKLE, 2004-05 PRESIDENT OF SISTERS IN CRIME, BESTSELLING AUTHOR OF THE THOROUGHLY SOUTHERN MYSTERY SERIES "Nehring's delightful novel features history and romance with murder thrown in. Who would have imagined an Elderhostel could be so dangerous?"

J.M. HAYES, AUTHOR OF *PLAINS CRAZY*, *PRAIRIE GOTHIC*, AND *MAD DOG & ENGLISHMAN* "The treasure here is Radine Trees Nehring and her plucky crime solver, Carrie Culpeper McCrite."

DR. DOJELO C. RUSSELL, PROGRAM COORDINATOR, UNIVERSITY OF ARKANSAS ELDERHOSTEL PROGRAMS IN HOT SPRINGS, ARK. "The characters are as alive as present-day Hot Springs."

MUSIC TO DIE FOR BY RADINE TREES NEHRING

Carrie and Henry's special vacation at the Ozark Folk Center in Stone County, Arkansas, is cancelled by kidnapping and murder.

LIBRARY JOURNAL "As inviting as an episode of *Murder, She Wrote*, this follow-up to Nehring's Macavity Award-nominated *A Valley to Die For* delivers a good, old-fashioned whodunit that should please any fan of Christian cozies."

THE OKLAHOMAN "The Ozark Folk Center...is the setting for the second in a series of 'to die for' mysteries by a former

Oklahoman who obviously loves the Ozarks..." (REVIEWED BY KAY DYER)

THE TULSA WORLD "...hooks [readers] with a story they can't put down." (REVIEWED BY JUDY RANDLE)

MIDWEST BOOK REVIEW "...[leaves] the reader sighing in satisfaction." (REVIEWED BY SHELLEY GLODOWSKI)

MYSTERY SCENE MAGAZINE "A nicely woven cozy by a writer who knows both the music and the hill people of Arkansas." (REVIEWED BY MARY V. WELK)

COZIES, CAPERS & CRIMES "In this character-driven story, heroes have their values straight and fight for what they believe in." (REVIEWED BY VERNA SUIT)

I LOVE A MYSTERY "Highly recommended." (REVIEWED BY EDEN EMBLER)

OZARKS MONTHLY "Happily, rumplyness takes nothing away from the cleverness of gray-haired heroine Carrie McCrite..." (REVIEWED BY LEE KIRK)

GRAVETTE NEWS HERALD "Action, plot twists and wonderful characters..." (REVIEWED BY GAYLE WILLIAMS)

THE BENTON COUNTY DAILY RECORD "...Nehring's specialties— intrigue and suspense, unique characters and situations—all set in the gorgeous Ozarks."

AMI ELIZABETH REEVES, AUTHOR OF *NEXT OF KIN* "With an ear for dialect and an eye for the beauty of her natural surroundings, Nehring brings a strong sense of place to the twists and turns that ensue while searching for the child."

JOE DAVID RICE, ARKANSAS TOURISM DIRECTOR "...a compelling read."

BARBARA BRETT, AUTHOR OF *BETWEEN TWO ETERNITIES* AND, WITH HY BRETT, *PROMISES TO KEEP* "...murder and mayhem in perfect pitch!"

JULIE WRAY HERMAN, AUTHOR OF THE THREE DIRTY WOMEN GARDENING MYSTERY SERIES "Endearing characters make you want to come back to visit soon!"

MARY GILLIHAN, HARMONY MUSICIAN; PARK INTERPRETER AND ELDERHOSTEL COORDINATOR, OZARK FOLK CENTER STATE PARK "It was such fun to read about our Ozark Folk Center and picture where *the murder* took place."

———

A VALLEY TO DIE FOR BY RADINE TREES NEHRING

Carrie McCrite and her neighbors are fighting to save their beloved Ozark valley from becoming a stone quarry. But when someone decides that one of them should die, Carrie must uncover and destroy the darkness swirling in the valley.

LIBRARY JOURNAL "With flair, Nehring, an award-winning Arkansas writer, launches a cozy series that will appeal to mystery readers..."

THE TULSA WORLD "The skill...the character development, the place, the pace and the action tell the true story." (REVIEWED BY MICHELE PATTERSON)

SOUTHERN SCRIBE "...a warm and enchanting tale. Carrie is charming as a woman who wants to be recognized as spunky, independent, and a hero. Casting the book in the Ozarks is... well, icing on the cake." (REVIEWED BY ROBERT L. HALL)

FORT SMITH TIMES RECORD "...a delightful mystery with appealing characters fighting for a cause. Throughout the story I grew all the more attached to Carrie, marveling at her strong faith and silently chastising her for her stubbornness. A...bonus is Carrie's cooking." (REVIEWED BY TINA DALE)

GRAVETTE NEWS HERALD "...kept my heart pounding...a page turner with no easy stopping places." (REVIEWED BY GAYLE WILLIAMS)

THE BOOKWATCH "...a smoothly written novel that grips the reader's attention from first page to last, and documents Radine Trees Nehring as a mystery writer whose imagination and talent will win her a large and dedicated readership."

I LOVE A MYSTERY "The suspense is grabbing, but the book is as relaxing as living alone in the forest... Very highly recommended." (REVIEWED BY EDEN EMBLER)

JANE HOOPER, PROPRIETOR OF SHERLOCK'S HOME BOOKSTORE "Weeks later, I'm still thinking about the book and characters. I can't wait for the next in the series."

CAROLYN HART, AUTHOR OF THE DEATH ON DEMAND AND HENRIE O MYSTERIES "A pleasure awaits mystery lovers."

DR. FRED PFISTER, EDITOR OF *THE OZARKS MOUNTAINEER* "It's great to read fiction about the Ozarks that rings true."

MIKE FLYNN, PRODUCER AND HOST OF THE *FOLK SAMPLER*, HEARD WEEKLY ON PUBLIC RADIO "...a fascinating mystery that gets better and better as the pages roll."

DEAR EARTH: A LOVE LETTER FROM SPRING HOLLOW BY RADINE TREES NEHRING

The unforgettable chronicle of a couple who traded secure jobs and the rat race for a life of simplicity and quiet joy.

BOOKLIST "Read it and dream."

Midwest Book Review "This compelling story traces their transitional experiences, presenting an endearing account."

Dr. Neil Compton (conservastionist and Pulitzer Prize nominee for *The Battle for the Buffalo River*) "An engrossing account of the ups and downs of a couple who cast aside the big city life for life in the hills. Nehring's book is a must!"

Mike Flynn (producer and host, "Folk Sampler," National Public Radio) "You should give this book to everyone you love, particularly to the young, so they can learn the things that Radine and John learned on their journey to the Ozarks."

Marvin Baker, Ph.D. (past Regional Vice President, Sierra Club) "There is inspiration here for all who contemplate making a change in living that brings one closer to the natural world."

David T. Nolan (President, Northwest Arkansas Audubon Society) "An interesting adventure in moving, not of physically moving the body, but of moving the mind."

A Clear North Light by Laurel Schunk

Petras Simonaitis is a struggling Lithuanian artisan. When his sister dies, perhaps at the hands of a cruel Baron, Petras must try to protect Rima, the woman he loves, from the same fate. But is he strong enough?

Library Journal "Schunk solidly launches a new 'Lithuanian' trilogy, following one family's triumphs and tragedies through the generations."

Booklist "Schunk, author of the well-regarded coming-of-age story *Black and Secret Midnight* (1998), drops back to

1938 with *A Clear North Light*, the first installment of her Lithuanian Trilogy."

NWSBRFS **(WICHITA PRESS WOMEN, INC.)** "...notable as much for its excellent character development as for its story line... Good reading..."

GRETCHEN SPRAGUE, AUTHOR OF *MAQUETTE FOR MURDER* "...dramatically illuminates the effect of deadly global politics on the private lives of all-too-human individuals caught up in events not of their making."

JAMES D. YODER, AUTHOR OF *LUCY OF THE TRAIL OF TEARS* "...pulls one into an historical drama with excitement and moral persuasiveness as Petras fights and searches for faith, meaning, and love..."

UNDER THE WOLF'S HEAD BY KATE CAMERON

All Callie Bagley wants is to be left alone to garden. But her plans for solitude are interrupted when a dead body shows up nearly on her back step.

GRIT: AMERICAN LIFE & TRADITIONS "You'll laugh at the sisters' relationship and grow to love the two women just as Callista's plants grow through her loving care."

PUBLISHERS WEEKLY "The gardening tips seeded throughout the narrative are a clever ploy, echoing the inclusion of cooking tips in the ever-popular culinary mysteries..."

LIBRARY JOURNAL "Plenty of gardening filler and allusions to inept local law enforcement lighten the atmosphere, as do the often humorous sisterly 'fights' and the speedy prose."

Norwich Bulletin "Schunk in the past has tackled child abuse and racism; her first gardening mystery provides a message about ageism and the value placed on elderly lives..."

The Charlotte Austin Review "Highly recommended." (REVIEWED BY NANCY MEHL)

About.com "...a wonderful new release..." (REVIEWED BY RENIE DUGWYLER)

The Bookdragon Review "...evokes in the reader an understanding of the atmosphere of a small town, where everyone is important and interesting." (REVIEWED BY RICHARD ROYCE)

NWSBRFS (Wichita Press Women, Inc.) "...a quick and pleasant read..."

James D. Yoder, author of *Black Spider Over Tiegenhof* "Kate Cameron brings this murder mystery to a finale, murders solved, villains implicated and captured, with the added bonus, protagonist Callie Bagley discovers new love in her life."

Death in Exile by Laurel Schunk

The Regency is noted for its gaiety, but sometimes the sparkling repartee covers darker things, like murder. Lord Wentworth and Anna Kate work to save their friend Diana from death in exile.

Library Journal "What could have been a straightforward Regency romance is elevated by apt social commentary in this offering from Schunk..."

The Pilot "Schunk is a good writer who has a good grasp of story and character."

THE CHARLOTTE AUSTIN REVIEW "This beautifully written Regency novel...will throw you into another time, and you won't want to leave." (REVIEWED BY NANCY MEHL)

MURDER: PAST TENSE (THE HIST. MYS. APPREC. SOC.) "Laurel Schunk is a masterful storyteller."

BLACK AND SECRET MIDNIGHT BY LAUREL SCHUNK

Murder in the South in the 1950's. Are Beth Anne's innocent questions about racism precipitating the murders?

LIBRARY JOURNAL "Beth Anne's appealing child's-eye view of the world and the subtle Christian message should make this appealing to fans of Christian and mainstream mysteries."

PUBLISHERS WEEKLY "Beth Anne is at times touchingly naive..."

SMALL PRESS BOOK REVIEW "...a memorable picture of racism that is variously stark and nuanced."

THE PILOT "...a good look at racial relations in the south...with a mysterious twist."

MURDER: PAST TENSE (THE HIST. MYS. APPREC. SOC.) "The story is so gripping that I worried [Beth Anne] would be killed before the end."

NWSBRFS (WICHITA PRESS WOMEN, INC.) "...Schunk's adult novels are serious, skillfully crafted works."

THE CHARLOTTE AUSTIN REVIEW "...a light in the darkness and a novel to sink your teeth and your heart into." (REVIEWED BY NANCY MEHL)

AMAZON.COM "...a great regional mystery that will excite fans with its twists and turns." (REVIEWED BY HARRIET KLAUSNER)

DOROTHYL "...skillfully mixes a story of segregation in the South and deep, dark family secrets with the plot of Shakespeare's 'MacBeth' in a very unique way." (REVIEWED BY TOM GRIFFITH)

SANDY DENGLER, AUTHOR OF *THE QUICK AND THE DEAD* "Mac-Beth and mayhem in the 50s. What a mix! I love Ms. Schunk's characters, and I remember the milieu all too well. It was the era you love to hate, beautifully brought to life."

LINDA HALL, AUTHOR OF *MARGARET'S PEACE* "Indicative of life in the South in the 1950s when racism and bigotry were around every frightening corner, *Black and Secret Midnight* is a great mystery with plenty of foreshadowing, clues, and red herrings to keep you reading far into the night."

THE VOICE HE LOVED BY LAUREL SCHUNK

Paige Brookings has traded her career as a New York model for a less glamorous life in Wichita, Kansas. Now she's being stalked. Can she protect herself from an anonymous madman?

THE CHARLOTTE AUSTIN REVIEW "...a masterful tale that reaches into the inner workings of a bruised and battered psyche, while keeping the plot moving at a breathless pace." (REVIEWED BY NANCY MEHL)

THE HEART OF MATTHEW JADE BY RALPH ALLEN
(AVAILABLE ONLY FROM ST KITTS PRESS)

As Matthew Jade ministers to the lost and broken, three inmates die. Who is the killer, and who will be the next victim in the cages of Coffin County Jail?

PUBLISHERS WEEKLY "...a compassionate view into religious, familial and romantic love..."

KEVIN PATRICK, CNET RADIO, SAN FRANCISCO "Fabulous!"

THE MIDWEST BOOK REVIEW "...an obliging and magnificently written mystery which is as entertaining as it is ultimately inspiring."

THE EAGLE "...Allen's book will inspire many who believe in the power of faith — and enjoy a good story."

THE CHARLOTTE AUSTIN REVIEW "...an eye-opener. *The Heart of Matthew Jade* is a compelling novel that will stay with you long after you put it down." (REVIEWED BY NANCY MEHL)

THE BOOKDRAGON REVIEW "...this novel's strength is in the behind the scenes glimpses of faith behind bars." (REVIEWED BY MELANIE C. DUNCAN)

THE LANTERN "...destined to become a classic. Its mixture of love and hate, religion and fallacy grabs readers from the very beginning and never lets them go."

LAUREL SCHUNK, AUTHOR OF *BLACK AND SECRET MIDNIGHT* "This compelling story chronicles the faith journey of a simple accountant from his sanitized office building into the maw of Hell as chaplain in a county jail."

HYÆNAS BY SANDY DENGLER
(AVAILABLE ONLY FROM ST KITTS PRESS)

Gar, shaman of his clan of Neanderthals, must discover who killed a rival clansman. And a mysterious stranger with the heart of strength of a hyæna follows him every step of the way.

LIBRARY JOURNAL "Highly recommended."

INTERNET BOOKWATCH (THE MIDWEST BOOK REVIEW) "...a terrific murder mystery and a work of unique, flawless written exploration of prehistoric antiquity."

THE CHARLOTTE AUSTIN REVIEW "Dengler has crafted a masterpiece. *Hyaenas* proves that there are still new slants to the mystery genre." (REVIEWED BY NANCY MEHL)

AMAZON.COM "For anyone who wants something a bit different with their mysteries, *Hyaenas* is the answer, hopefully with future novels starring Gar and company." (REVIEWED BY HARRIET KLAUSNER)

DOROTHYL "...I had a hard time putting the book down when I needed to do some work." (REVIEWED BY TOM GRIFFITH)

PAT RUSHFORD, AUTHOR OF THE HELEN BRADLEY MYSTERIES "Dengler is masterful at creating characters that come alive in any era."